Neil MacDonald's debut novel introduces an exciting talent. The book won two prizes during its development, the Plot of Gold and a Cinnamon Press mentorship.

He has also published short stories in magazines including *Structo* and *Gold Dust* as well as articles about writing and six books on human rights and international aid. Born in Scotland and raised in Jamaica he has lived and worked in England, the USA, South Africa, and now lives in a cottage in Surrey with his wife and the two obligatory dogs.

See more of his work at:
www.neilmacdonaldauthor.com

THE
TEARS
OF
BOABDIL

Neil MacDonald

Copyright © 2020 Neil MacDonald

The moral right of the author has been asserted.

Apart from any fair dealing for the purposes of research or private study, or criticism or review, as permitted under the Copyright, Designs and Patents Act 1988, this publication may only be reproduced, stored or transmitted, in any form or by any means, with the prior permission in writing of the publishers, or in the case of reprographic reproduction in accordance with the terms of licences issued by the Copyright Licensing Agency. Enquiries concerning reproduction outside those terms should be sent to the publishers.

This is a work of fiction. Names, characters, businesses, places, events and incidents are either the products of the author's imagination or used in a fictitious manner. Any resemblance to actual persons, living or dead, or actual events is purely coincidental.

Matador
9 Priory Business Park,
Wistow Road, Kibworth Beauchamp,
Leicestershire. LE8 0RX
Tel: 0116 279 2299
Email: books@troubador.co.uk
Web: www.troubador.co.uk/matador
Twitter: @matadorbooks

ISBN 978 1800460 188

British Library Cataloguing in Publication Data.
A catalogue record for this book is available from the British Library.

Printed and bound in the UK by TJ Books Limited, Padstow, Cornwall
Typeset in 11pt Adobe Garamond Pro by Troubador Publishing Ltd, Leicester, UK

Matador is an imprint of Troubador Publishing Ltd

To Marian

CHAPTER 1

Waiting is the mother of change. The hard wooden bench aches my buttocks, making a torment of the wait. These seats assert the court's grandeur, offering only the most austere comfort. I squirm, and scratch my beard. But the skin is tender and newly-shaven. Change. I am no longer bearded, no longer Zami.

Part of what I will reveal is a lie. Or a story, which is much the same thing, since I'm not sure truth exists. You may think you'll be able to figure out which bits are untrue, but I should warn you, I'm an excellent liar. Spinning yarns is my business. Even when it's done with love. Can you love those to whom you lie? I believe you can because I have. You may think that makes me a bad person. Whether I am the hero or the villain of this tale, you will decide.

With the benefit of hindsight, I'm free to range over the whole of space and time. This allows me to explore not just what happened, but what it meant. I'm not going to narrate this exactly as it happened, step-by-step, because the roots of things often lie in the past, and they also lie in the future. Our hopes and plans shape what happens. So,

I'll try to craft the tale to make best sense of it. Where to begin?

The swing doors to the waiting room open and she is there. My heart lurches.

Ayesha first enters my story through the humble medium of trade goods – a pack of cigarettes and a bottle of water. She stood in shadow behind the counter when I entered the corner shop, and only when I approached did I see her features. There was nothing special about her, except maybe a hint of sadness in the large obsidian eyes, etched with kohl. The small mystery of that melancholy was strangely attractive. Perhaps spending all day tending the shop might make anyone a little sad. The lustre of the hair, which I later learned she brushed for half an hour every morning, was not visible, for she covered it with a black hijab trimmed in gold.

There was no sign of her brothers, Rashid and Afaq, in the shop. Perhaps they were in the flat upstairs, but I was certain I could find them in the mosque at the *Zuhr* noon prayer. The walk wasn't far. I'd studied the map that came with the file.

These first moments were always exhilarating. When you became another person and entered the chase. Nerves become better, muscles more, I sensed a pulse at my temple. Even the anxiety about being unmasked was a buzz. Could she tell who I was? No, of course not.

The shop was sandwiched between an international money transfer office and a beauty salon in a down-at-heel back street. Crates of fruit and vegetables were stacked chaotically over the pavement, ripening in the spring sunshine. Inside was a jumble of snacks, tins and bottles, brand-name baked beans jostling with exotic canned goods labelled in Urdu. The scent of spices mingled with that of mildew.

Ayesha's face transformed as I plonked the bottle of water on the counter. The transaction flipped a switch somewhere, and the marionette came to life. Gone was the sadness, and a smile of welcome made her radiant. White teeth, and eyes from which the light danced.

"Will there be anything else?" Those were the first words she spoke to me.

"A packet of cigarettes, please, sister," I said, leaning across the counter towards the cigarettes and asked for my brand. I caught her perfume – flowers, and underneath that her own essence of rich loam.

"Oh, you're a Muslim?" She had picked up on the "sister" and her smile broadened as she included me in her world.

"Yes, sister, I am, praise be to Allah."

As she turned in profile to reach for the cigarettes, I was struck by the disproportionate angularity of her nose. When she turned back to face me, her long equine head reverted again to perfect balance.

This part of the story had not yet happened, but I always hated it when Ayesha turned away from me. If I am honest, it wasn't just because of the rejection – it was my churlish Anglo Saxon ideal of beauty marred by her South Asian nose. In some ways, we are all perhaps unreconstructed racists. Whenever possible, I approached Ayesha head-on. And head-on was how she approached life.

"There you go, brother."

To prolong the encounter would have been wrong, but at least I was in and working. For now, I thanked her and left the shop, tearing the plastic ring off the neck of the bottle. I paused to drop the ring and the cellophane wrapping of the cigarette pack into a rubbish bin. As I looked up the street towards the mosque, I savoured the gurgle of water down my throat and the first hit of nicotine since I got off the train from London, new to town and eager to be in action.

The action has led to unexpected places, to this courtroom. Ayesha glares and pointedly sits on the far side of the room. But this was all for her. The only way I knew how to protect her.

Time in stories doesn't run in a straight line from start to finish, and depending on where you start, the meaning changes. Rashid and Afaq could provide another beginning.

As the plaintive call to prayer reverberated around the labyrinth of terraced streets, the mosque seemed to tell a story about the interweaving of past and present. Its architecture was a confection of neo-classical and Indo-European. The central onion dome topped a Bargate stone grand portico of purest white, detailed in turquoise and umber. To either side pavilions bore canopied pinnacles at the corners.

As I joined the stream of worshippers, passed through the doors and made my ablutions, some favoured me with curious glances. White Muslims are still not common, but I sensed no hostility as I knelt, facing Mecca. I recognised Rashid and Afaq, kneeling near the front. The photos on the file didn't do them justice. They were handsome men.

The beat of my heart sounded in my ears, a dull thud of pressure. Not at all like the whoosh of medical equipment on the telly. Air sighed from my nostrils. In and out. I inhaled and held the breath. Then released it, slow and sure. My heartbeat slowed, the pulse in my ears steadied.

Rashid was wearing a green shirt, the colour bright and sharp, peculiarly vibrant. I watched the cotton stretch over a broad back as he bent his head to the ground. A fly settled on my arm and I didn't brush it off, enjoying the iridescence of its wings.

No mistakes now. Take it slow. Don't blow it. When the prayers ended, I didn't try to strike up acquaintance with the brothers. Respect is the currency on which groups run, respect and shared ideals. You earn your place, and I still needed to secure mine.

Worshippers spilled from the mosque into the spring sunshine, and a knot of eager friends surrounded Rashid. To some he smiled and inclined his head, to others he offered a word. One he clapped on the shoulder, leaning in close to share a confidence, and I saw the man grow a little straighter, squaring his shoulders. The sexes prayed separately, and now the women emerged. Rashid's wife, holding a child by the hand, joined him, and he put his arm around her without embarrassment, then lifted the laughing boy high into the air.

The file told me Rashid was a man of some standing, a fine school teacher. You didn't just go up to him and say hello. Not if you wanted to avoid suspicion.

Or perhaps the story really starts a thousand miles south in Granada where Ayesha and I first lay together.

CHAPTER 2

But again, I am getting ahead of my story. If I am to recount this successfully, perhaps it would be safer to remove myself from the tale and tell it dispassionately of another man. That will allow me to rehearse the evidence and put the events into a sensible order.

All of this happened to someone else. His name is now Zami. That's the name I took when I spoke the words of conversion "*Ashadu an la ilaha illa Allah, wa ashadu Mohammad rasoolu Allah*" – "I bear witness there is no god but Allah, and Mohammad is his messenger."

When you try on another identity, like a jacket in a shop, there is the oddest feeling. Part sadness as you lose yourself, but joy also as you puff out your chest and animate the freedom of your new story. Zami was like that for me. He was fearless and unburdened by my doubts, his heart pure, sure of his triumph, and unconcerned about whether he was worthy of love. If he had any anxieties, they amounted to no more than the risk of being unmasked.

The story might start a thousand miles south in Granada where Ayesha and Zami first lay together. Granada, with its sharp Mediterranean light and its deep comforting shadows cooled by the breeze off the Sierra Nevada, the snowy mountains.

The history of Moorish Spain, Al Andalus, fascinated Ayesha, and her passion infected Zami. The great Kings and Andalusian scholars were rock stars to her. Over coffee in their hideaway, she breathed their names like incantations. Until he met her, Zami had never heard of any of these people.

"It makes me so proud to be a Muslim," she said as the plane carried them over Spain. "We once ruled in Europe in a caliphate that was tolerant and cultured, in a sea of barbaric Christian kingdoms."

Most of all, Ayesha was enthralled by Andalusian society's tolerance. She told him Muslims, Jews, and Christians co-existed in harmony.

Rashid and Afaq didn't feel at all the same way about Al Andalus. They were hard line. They dismissed Moorish Spain with contempt as a false caliphate. It tolerated *kufars*, a nasty name for unbelievers, and embraced Greek learning and Jewish scholarship, so by definition the civilisation wasn't Islamic.

And yet, two nicer blokes you could never meet. Zami grew to like them immensely – shirt-off-their-back types. Except for the tiny problem of their obsession with killing. Well, to be fair, they hadn't blown anything up, but they talked a lot about holy war.

Ayesha once told Zami that goodness is a solid whereas evil is a liquid. You need a little evil in you, she said, to weather the edges off the goodness, otherwise it cuts the heart.

She may have been right. Her brothers' talk of *jihad* may have been something sinister, or it may just have been young bloods posturing. Only the court case will tell.

Al Andalus existed a long time ago. Moslem Spain ended in 1492, the year Columbus sailed for the Americas. Ayesha told Zami that Boabdil, the last Sultan of Granada, surrendered his city to the Catholic Monarchs, Ferdinand and Isabella, stopped at a high place, looked back, and shed a tear.

The tale also recounts that his battle-axe of a mother chastised him, "You do well to weep like a woman for what you failed to defend as a man." But that seemed a shitty thing for a mother to say to her son in those circumstances, so Zami reckoned that bit must have been invented.

When Ayesha and Zami visited Granada, they made a pilgrimage to the mountain pass in the Sierra Nevada where Boabdil is said to have shed his tear. To this day, the spot is called the *Suspiro del Moro,* the Moor's Sigh. Granada is interwoven with the tale that Zami crafted for Ayesha's delight. He believed the past shapes the present, and the present, in its turn, fashions what we believe to be history. Thus does the future shape the past.

"Tell me the Don Vincent story," Ayesha would demand, as she lay in Zami's arms. "Tell it again."

Her eyes would shine with the anticipation of the familiar. For the tale was hers. And he would gladly retell it, for the tale was his too. His name was Vince before he became Zami. And the story was one of conquest that he crafted to woo her.

"Well," Zami would begin. "Don Vincent is a student from Salamanca, a well-born lad, clever, charming, and handsome. In the summers, he goes wandering the roads of Iberia, moving from town to town with his lute, singing to the crowds, and reciting stories. Throughout the land, his voice has no equal, neither in Catholic Spain, nor among the Moors."

Zami's voice, tender and deep, seemed to captivate Ayesha.

"And then he arrived in Granada," she said.

"And then he arrived in Granada," Zami agreed.
"Where he met Ayesha," she added.
"Not yet, not yet."

Don Vincent put down his pack, gazed up at the palace and then back at the walled city quarter. The late afternoon lay warm and lazy as a stray dog in the esplanade by the Darro River. A contented sigh rustled the leaves of the trees shading the promenade, and everything was slow. This valley floor was a place of ease and ampleness. It opened between the bulk of the Alhambra fortress to the south and the steeply rising alleys of the Al-bayyazin to the north.

This was another realm, last bastion of the embattled Moors, exotic and forbidden. The scent of spices perfumed the air that carried the sound of tongues from across the known world. Everything around Don Vincent was new and exciting. Different banners flew over the Alhambra and the Al-bayyazin. Whose flags they were, he did not recognise, but that this was a divided city, he had no doubt.

"The rival banners of Sultan Abu Hassan, and of his son, Boabdil," said Ayesha.

"Hush, habibti. Let the tale unfold," Zami chided. "Stories have their own time, and Don Vincent is new to town. He knows nothing."

"But the listener knows," Ayesha said. "In our world, we move from cause to effect. But stories are different. They move from effect back to cause – they are written backwards. Everything results from the ending."

"But they are listened to forwards," Zami said. "The listener doesn't know in advance what the ending is."

Ayesha wasn't aware of it, but she didn't yet know the end of Don Vincent's story. Zami hadn't told her everything. But she quieted and listened again.

Don Vincent bought a pot of ale, cool from its earthenware vessel, and rested in the sun between the fortress and the citadel. People from all over the world passed him by – proud Arabs, adventurous Christians from the North, Jews in their skullcaps, and swarthy Berbers from North Africa. Some stopped, as he did, on the riverside, talking arm in arm, or simply relaxing. But most were going about their business. A group of craftsmen with their tools crossed the bridge, heading towards the Alhambra. A trader's donkey train snaked along the cobbles and in through an open gate into the Al-bayyazin.

Where there are traders, there are buyers, Don Vincent reasoned, and where there are buyers, there are crowds who will give a coin for a song or a tale. He shouldered his pack and followed the donkeys into the town.

"But," said Ayesha, "he meets his Ayesha at the Alhambra."

"Yes," Zami agreed, "but not yet. First, he has to enter the old city."

Beyond the gate was a broad, open thoroughfare that narrowed to an alley where it climbed the hill. The upper stories of houses, with porticoes leaning over the street, embraced it on either side. The trader's train plodded round a corner, and Don Vincent followed. Around that bend was a marvel – a world composed of smell and sound. The scent of cardamom and of nutmeg, the shouts of hawkers advertising their wares and customers bargaining. Spices, and silks, oils and unguents, the air itself seemed alive with depth and texture, woven through the seething crowd.

"Señor, I see you are a gentleman. Time is running out."

Don Vincent turned. The voice came from an old man, seated cross legged at a low table on the street. A purple silk turban wrapped his head, and light flashed from the rings that adorned every finger.

"Excuse me?" Don Vincent answered in passable Arabic.

"Time, señor, it's running out. Perhaps the gentleman would care to buy some more." The vendor upended an hourglass and Don Vincent watched the sand trickle through the constriction. He was mesmerised by the pile at the bottom, growing grain by grain. Time would be a fine thing to possess.

Though he was sure he was being tricked, he asked, "How much?"

"A glass of time, señor, for one bottle of luck."

He had to laugh at that. "And where might I get a bottle of luck?"

"At the far end of the street of potions, señor." The merchant pointed down the street. "Ask for Sandor, tell him Adil sent you."

Don Vincent trekked down the narrow alley where Adil pointed, ducking around snake charmers and jugglers, carried along by the surge and susurration of the crowd. The entry to the alley blazed with sudden light as the early evening sun penetrated it. Shadows fled, and warmth licked Don Vincent's cheek. He squinted at a world suddenly reduced to silhouette in the glare.

Sandor, squatting on a faded carpet surrounded by crystal phials, was identifiable as a Jew from his yarmulke. He was every bit as youthful and flamboyant as Adil was old and wrinkled. It was as if their roles were reversed – this man seemed the purveyor of eternal youth, while Adil with his fine jewellery smacked of good fortune.

"You sell luck?"

"Sandor Fisher at your service. Yes, I sell luck, the best in the business, all the way from Damascus. But, if I may be so bold, you don't look to me like a gentleman who needs any luck."

"I have my share," Don Vincent answered, "but Adil sent me, and he will only sell time in exchange for luck."

"Ah." Sandor's face clouded. "My profound apologies, but I sell luck only in exchange for time. One glass of time will buy you a bottle of luck. If you have no time, I am afraid we will be unable to conduct any business."

"But this is absurd," Don Vincent said.

"Yes, it is rather. But then, when you think about it, life is a little absurd. There is nothing I can do about that."

In exasperation, Don Vincent stumped back down the street. Adil called as he passed, "Time is running out."

The traveller found plain lodgings near the Al-bayyazin gate and set off to explore the other side of the river. Passing a magnificent bath house, he pondered the strange Muslim habit of regular bathing, sure that it invited disease. Though water cleansed the body's stench, it opened the pores allowing infection to enter.

The road now bent and ran steeply up the hill towards the Alhambra fortress palace. Guards stopped Don Vincent at an arched gate in the wall encircling the complex. He trudged round the perimeter, passing a succession of guard towers, whose archers peered down at him suspiciously, but he found no other entry.

He was about to give up when he spotted a soldier standing ramrod-stiff by a small tower, which was swaddled in mist. Don Vincent could not make out his features because the sinking sun turned him into a silhouette, hazy in the fog. But, even so, it was clear the soldier was dressed in the armour of Castile. The distinctive kettle helmet was unmistakable.

Don Vincent addressed him in Spanish.

"*Buenas tardes, amigo.*"

"*Buenas tardes, señor. Puede usted ayudarme* – can you help me?" The soldier grasped Don Vincent's arm. "Please, for the love of God."

The soldier's fingers seemed to sink into Don Vincent's arm, as if they were not made of the same substance. Alarmed, he snatched his arm away and replied, "If it's within my power."

"Please listen to me, what I have to tell you may sound incredible, but please listen until the end."

Don Vincent nodded and listened in silence, arms folded.

"I went to war for His Majesty, King Alfonso VI of Castile. The battle was terrible, the defeat total. They captured me at Sagrajas."

"But that was in 1086." Don Vincent was incredulous. "That was four hundred years ago,"

The soldier held up his hand. "Patience, señor, I will explain. I was taken prisoner, and my punishment was to stand guard over this treasure, a great Moorish treasure, that lies within this tower."

Don Vincent came alert, like a pointer. "A treasure? What is it?"

"I do not know, señor. I only know it is something they do not wish to fall into Christian hands. They cast a spell on me, and on the treasure, and the whole turret, on St. John's Eve."

"But it is St. John's Eve today!"

"Yes, señor, and that is why you're able to see me. I and the tower appear only on St John's Eve. And only once every hundred years." The soldier hung his head in sadness. "I have been condemned to this miserable existence for the last four hundred years."

"How can I free you from this spell?"

"You have only to enter the tower and I shall at last be free to rest my ancient bones. Half of the treasure is yours if you will but save me."

"And the other half?"

"Be kind. I will need something for myself."

Don Vincent strode to the foot of the tower. "I will save you, my man. Let me in."

"Would that I could, señor. But the door opens only for a fasting priest and a chaste maiden. Be quick, I beg you, find both and return here. I cannot bear to wake up yet again to find another hundred years has passed."

Don Vincent agreed and scrambled down the hill and back to the Al-bayyazin. Though Granada was a Muslim city, Christians were free to worship according to their religion, and priests could be found. Whether there were chaste girls, Don Vincent was less certain, for he had heard the Granadinos loved their pleasure.

He passed from inn to stable, from church to street, seeking the two keys to the treasure.

CHAPTER 3

Zami approached his guarded tower with caution. Every day, he rose, breakfasted, visited the corner shop, went to mosque, put himself about a bit. Not having to shave saved time in the morning. He was eating into his stock of time, and it made him nervous. Soon, he would have to check-in.

He told himself he frequented the corner shop, hoping to run into Rashid and Afaq. It was never likely. Rashid didn't live with the family above the shop. Afaq still lived at home, but studied. Neither brother inhabited the shop much.

Ayesha served there every day except Wednesdays, sometimes with an elderly whiskered gentleman in a *shalwar kameez* who must have been her father. Often, she was alone. Zami bought cigarettes, water, and newspapers he discarded unread.

He sought a way to get close to the family, progressing from "good morning, sister" to "how are you today?" as she came to recognise him. They discussed the weather as Brits do. "Looks like a nice day today," he'd say, and she would agree that it was most clement.

Over time, she learned what brand he smoked, and would present him with the pack and a bright smile. They became polite and cordial with each other, but he got no closer to the family. A good Muslim, her upbringing forbade entertaining a strange man.

Time before he had to report was running out. If only he could borrow some. On the sands of the future lay nothing but time, evaporating crusty in the sun. The past too was replete with the stuff, but already used and full of events.

To get from here to there, you need only find the story that connects the two. In the future, he would befriend Ayesha, winning her trust, slow and sure. And so he did. Chats about the weather became discussion of events in the town and the imam's sermons at the mosque. And, at last, an exchange of confidences.

"I have two faces," she said, "the one I show the world, and the one for me. They are not the same."

He understood that. His smile was thin but freighted with sympathy. He said, "Exile makes sense when you realise you were never really at home in the first place."

Zami built up an overdraft with the future, against the security of his luck.

While he got to know their sister, he circled, attending the mosque regularly, leafing through literature at the *dawah* stall. Rashid and Afaq were not to be taken by main force, but by subtlety. He got himself noticed as a devout man by praying punctiliously and let them come to him.

The brothers were always there on the stall outside the mosque after Friday prayers, and sometimes on Saturdays in the town's market precinct.

Rain was threatening in a leaden sky the Friday Rashid first talked to him, as he examined a leaflet on The Meaning of the Kaliphate.

"You interested in the *Khilafah*, bruv?"

"Yeah," Zami replied. "It couldn't hardly be worse than what we've got now if we ran things on Islamic lines."

Rahid nodded. "Allah's law, not man's law, innit?"

The street argot concealed Rashid's education. Zami already knew he was an IT graduate and an admired science teacher, as well as a doting father and the mainstay of the local football league. He had his sister's obsidian eyes and sculpted features.

Zami's finger traced the words on the page. "*Jama'ah*, community, and *tawid*, unity. I like that."

"Time is running out," Afaq called to a passer-by. "Your Lord is most knowing of who has strayed from His way, and He is most knowing of who is rightly guided."

Afaq idolised his older brother, Zami knew.

"That's what *kufar* society don't have," Rashid agreed, "community. It's everyone for himself, innit? Competition, greed. There's a dark hole at the centre of British society, and in their souls. The important thing is what's in your soul, it ain't about what trainers you got."

Zami lit up his eyes. "That's so true, brother. An emptiness, yeah, it's empty."

"I seen you at the mosque, bruv. You new to town?"

"Yeah, just moved a couple of weeks ago, from London."

Afaq had cornered his next target, a sallow youth in a blue panjabi, and was inviting him to Islam. Zami listened in while telling Rashid about his move from the capital.

"You wanna come to our study circle, bruv, that's what you wanna do," Afaq was saying to the youth. "And learn all kinds of things about Islam you won't hear in the mosque."

Zami wanted to be invited to the study circle. He leaned over the stall as if to share a confidence with Afaq. He smelt the same scent of rich loam as he had from Ayesha in the shop.

"The imam's sermon today was interesting," Zami said. "Why pray if Allah already has a plan? But I wanted to understand more about His plan, not just that he tells us we should pray."

"Everything that happens has already been written a million years ago," Rashid explained. "We cannot change His mind by praying. He is a perfect Being and His decisions are the best choice. If He has chosen for me to die at forty, I cannot change His mind. We are ignorant and aren't aware of all the circumstances. The plan He has made for me is the best plan."

Zami nodded. This was exactly what he understood. He widened his eyes with eager innocence. "So then, why pray?"

"When we come to the Qu'ran we find the answers to why we should pray. He wrote everything, not in one book, but in two books."

"There's another book, besides the Holy Qu'ran?"

"I don't mean the Qu'ran, which the Angel Gabriel recited to the Prophet, peace be upon him. I mean the books that only Allah sees. In the first book, He wrote His plan in a conditional form. It is a rough draft. The book may say I will die at forty, but there's an if – I will die at forty if I don't take my medicine. So, that book changes."

"So we can change Allah's plans?" Zami thought this might be blasphemy.

"No," Rashid said. "The second book is the final form, the unchangeable one. It is the result of the first book, of my decision about whether to take care of my health. Allah already wrote it because He knows what my decision will be.

The day of judgement is in the unchangeable plan, but my life is in the first book. I can influence what happens."

"Wow!" Zami said. "I never thought of it like that. The imam didn't explain it that way either, but it makes sense."

"The imam is an old man from the old country. He don't understand Pakistan anymore, and he don't understand Britain. He don't really fit anywhere."

"Do any of us fit anywhere?" Zami asked.

Rashid gave him a look. That stare was long, silent, and searching. He felt he was being weighed.

"Maybe not," Rashid said at last, but offered Zami no invitation to the study group.

To push now would be a bad idea, so Zami took the pamphlet about the caliphate, and was going to leave when Afaq pushed another leaflet at him.

"Come to the protest, brother, tomorrow. Stand up for Muslims against the *kufar* law."

"What's it about?" Zami asked.

"Police brutality, you get me? Armed coppers broke into the Iqbal's house. Like, trashed the place. Took away Abdul Bari and Fouad and their computers and books and stuff. Mrs Iqbal is really twitched. We're having a march to the police station in protest to show them, *Inshallah*, they can't do that to us."

"Did they charge Abdul Bari and Fouad?"

"Nah, but they've still got them."

"Fucking filth," Zami said. "Yeah, I'll be there. They can't get away with that."

"We'll assemble in the park at five and then, like, march to the cop shop. Victoria Park, by the monument."

"Count me in," Zami said, pocketing the leaflets and strolling away from the mosque.

The gunmetal sky finally delivered on its threat as he reached the corner. A fat raindrop plopped at his feet and, a second later, another ran down his cheek. The weather did nothing to dampen his spirits. He turned up his collar as the downpour started. As he crossed the road, his feet channelled Gene Kelly. He splashed through a puddle, kicking up spray and whistling "Singing in the Rain".

His jubilation at the breakthrough lasted all the way to the town centre, a mixture of new high rise office and apartment blocks – all glass and concrete – and decaying Victorian shop terraces. Passing the long bleak wall of the railway station, he spotted a passenger emerging from the entrance. His body reacted before his consciousness registered the fact. An iron band clamped his chest and his throat constricted.

Tommy!

What the hell was Tommy doing here?

Zami ducked into a shop doorway and peered out at the man walking west down the lane. You couldn't even say that Tommy swaggered – he just walked with that damn confidence in his undeniable right to take up space in the world. And he took up his fair share of space. His bulk gave him a slight roll, like a sailor. But his stride was powerful and long.

Zami dried his palms against the thighs of his jeans and watched Tommy's retreating back. Even from behind, there was no mistaking Tommy. Though Zami took consolation from the distinct bald patch that had developed on the man's crown since seeing him last.

For the best part of fifteen years, Zami and Tommy had been orbiting each other like binary stars. Yet it was always Tommy who wrenched atmosphere from him, shining with the stolen material that should rightfully have been Zami's. Though, to be fair, their perpetual dance of death gave Zami added velocity.

But why was Tommy here? This was Zami's town.

CHAPTER 4

Don Vincent flashed like a comet across the Al-bayyazin, from the gate through twisting cobbled alleys to the hilltop *Mirador* and back. There were fasting priests aplenty in Granada on St. John's Eve, but none could be tempted to accompany Don Vincent to the Alhambra. In a coffee house, a swarthy night watchman guffawed at his plight. Girls thronged the streets and plazas, but their smiles were arch and knowing.

He felt the treasure slipping from his grasp. Only hours remained to enter the tower and rescue the soldier.

His looping through the steep streets slowed and his decaying orbit spiralled-in to the riverside promenade. Perhaps that place pulled him in due to the density of familiarity – this was where he had first lingered on arriving in Granada.

And there he encountered the priest, a corpulent old fellow with a woebegone expression, slouched on the embankment.

At first Don Vincent appealed to the man's Christian charity, urging him to help free the enchanted soldier.

"Would that I could," the priest replied. "But I am too weak with hunger to climb the hill to the palace."

At last, Don Vincent confessed the secret of the treasure. Avarice brightened the old eyes, and the holy man's lassitude vanished. Despite the decades that separated their ages, the younger man had to race to keep up with the priest.

"Hurry, hurry," the priest called over his shoulder, "there is no time to be lost. A Christian soul is in peril."

"Wait," Don Vincent cried. "We must also find a chaste girl."

"The Lord will provide, my son, for we are about His business."

They passed the gate of the Alhambra, and at that moment a comely maiden was leaving the palace with a basket of washing.

"The most beautiful woman, Don Vincent had ever seen in his life," breathed Ayesha.

"An angel," Zami agreed, *"with obsidian eyes and a slender, shapely body."* He crafted his words lovingly to ravish his listener.

The priest called the woman over. "My child, could you aid us? A man's life is at stake."

"Is she," Don Vincent whispered, "you know, chaste?"

"Oh yes, very," the holy man said. "She has refused me many times. Her name is Ayesha."

"You must help," said Don Vincent, "please."

She cast a doubtful glance at the priest.

"We have to save the soldier," Don Vincent urged. "Have pity."

She took some persuading, but she agreed, for she was moved by the tale, and the three skirted the palace wall until they came to the tower, where the soldier waited.

"Thank the Lord, señor, you are back," he said, when he recognised Don Vincent. "Be quick, there is not much time."

As if it had always been there but they just hadn't been looking right, a door appeared at the foot of the tower. It swung open to reveal age-worn spiral stairs leading to an upper chamber. In the centre of the room stood a stout wooden chest, bound in iron. A table stood beside the chest, empty except for a bowl of fruit.

The gluttonous priest's eyes darted from the strongbox to the bowl, Don Vincent's from the allure of the box to the beauty of the woman. She remained stilled as a pillar of salt, entranced by the magic.

The spell was ended and the iron bindings fell away from the chest. The young troubadour cranked back the ancient lid on rusty hinges to reveal gold coins, rubies, sapphires, and a silver crown of exquisite workmanship.

At the moment Don Vincent's hand reached out to grasp the crown, there came behind him a crunch. The priest had broken his fast, succumbing to the temptation of his hunger and bitten into an apple.

In that instant, the chest and the chamber disappeared. Don Vincent, Ayesha, and the priest found themselves again outside the tower. The door had vanished, and the soldier was nowhere to be seen, both wrenched into the realm of enchantment for another hundred years.

"Damn all priests." Don Vincent swore, but without rancour.

"But at least he won the girl," Ayesha would always say at this point.

"Not yet, habibti," Zami would say. "Ayesha is a chaste girl, and a Muslim, and he is a Catholic. Getting the girl was no easy task."

Over the next five weeks, Don Vincent tried every trick. He charmed and wheedled, serenaded and begged. It was all in vain. He forgot to eat, and grew pale from lack of sleep and food. The more Ayesha rebuffed him, the more he wanted her. She became an obsession. He would wait outside the palace gate until she came out with her washing and walk her home through the winding lanes of the Albayyazin. A dance of light in her eyes led him to believe his attentions were not unwelcome.

Ever and anon, when he was with Ayesha, he began to notice a swarthy night watchman by the name of Tomaz. For a while, Don Vincent thought this to be coincidence. But every time he saw Ayesha, Tomaz would appear, with his sailor's swagger and a grin that said he could have any woman he liked. Only in the mornings while his rival slept could Don Vincent, tormented by jealousy, catch her alone.

At first he simply desired to bed her, but, over weeks, this became yearning and then love. At last one afternoon, as she returned from her duties, he went down on one knee.

"I cannot, Vincent," she said. "I am a Muslim and you are a Catholic. You understand, Christian men are forbidden to marry Muslim women."

Tomaz, loitering in an alleyway, smirked. So desperate was Don Vincent to possess Ayesha that he renounced his religion and became a Muslim. In the end, she relented.

"And they lived happily ever after," said Ayesha.
"Uh, yes, ever after," said Zami.

And for Zami, winning the girl was no easy task. Though he was Muslim, his skin was white, as if the Christian Vince still lurked pale and skeletal beneath. In fact, Zami never set out to woo Ayesha at all. It was a bad idea. Rashid and Afaq would have been appalled, maybe even violent. The couple fell in love by accident, and by stealth. Always by stealth, hidden from Ayesha's family.

The opening of Zami's heart was the result of a simple question. He found her in the park after the demonstration. Many of the protesters had filtered back there to the starting place. Zami noticed her staring up at the sky with a rapt expression. His mind replaying the information from the protest, he failed to recognise her at first but drifted to her side, curious at what she was studying, and then recognised her smell.

"Hello," he said. "What's up there?"

She didn't turn to him but continued to peer upwards. "Why is the sky dark at night?"

"Because it's night time? Uh, there's no sun."

"But there are stars," she said. "If there were enough of them, the whole sky would be alight, wouldn't it brother Zami?"

"I suppose that's true."

"But since most of the sky isn't bright, there can't be enough stars," Ayesha said.

She pondered for a bit and then said. "So that must mean the universe isn't infinite. If it was, everywhere you looked, there would be a star."

Zami laughed. He liked philosophy, and few in his circle were philosophical.

"Maybe some are hidden by clouds," he said.

She looked around her, as if checking who might be watching them. "I should probably go."

"Don't go, sister. Not yet. I don't get to talk about the stars much."

She turned away, scanning the park, then looked at him. "You're a funny one." Her laugh was too shrill, a confection of anxiety and politeness.

"No, really, I'm interested."

In the days that followed they would talk often about astronomy, the nature of goodness, and duty. Perhaps she hadn't meant to. Perhaps for her it all began there too, just because he said he was interested.

The tension in her shoulders relaxed. Zami noticed how long her neck was.

"Did you know that it was Islamic astronomers who first questioned the Greek idea that the earth was the centre of the universe, long before Copernicus did?" she asked.

When Zami told her this was news to him, she added, "Yes, the Persian Tusi in the thirteenth century, and the Uzbeck, Ali Qushji, two hundred years later."

Her tone suggested she might have known them personally.

"Wow!" he said. "Did you know, when you look at the stars, you're looking back in time, because it takes the light so long to reach us? We're seeing the sky as it was, not as it is now."

"Yes, I know. It makes you feel very small, doesn't it?"

Though she was traditionally cloaked in an embroidered *shalwar kameez* and long red headscarf thrown over her shoulder, her manner was easy and she addressed him proudly, as an equal. Zami liked that. And, later, he fashioned a story in which he could like her more.

"See that star?" he said. "Maybe it's not there anymore, but we won't know for another five hundred years."

"And that one," Ayesha said, pointing. "Pow! Gone!"

They shook hands and stood together, snuffing out stars and giggling like teenagers. And that's probably when it started. Zami hadn't meant to fall in love with Ayesha – it was the worst thing that could have happened. From everyone's point of view.

Certainly, Rashid looked very displeased when he found the pair side by side sitting on the grass. He just folded his arms and fixed her with a stare. Ayesha scrambled up, embarrassed, as if caught out in a sin.

"Sorry, Zami, I have to go," she said. "It was good talking to you."

Rashid grabbed her arm and pulled her away, with a furious glare at Zami, then almost frogmarched her out of the park. Zami saw her shake her arm free and turn to face her brother at the gate. She was waving her hands as he leaned over her in threat.

"Oh shit," Zami muttered.

CHAPTER 5

Bad luck followed Zami. The brothers remained angry. After the midday prayer, Rashid ignored him, turning his head away, though Afaq nodded in his direction. But even Afaq's mouth was drawn into a tight line.

Shit!

Everything had been going so well. At the police station protest, he had moved close to Afaq and chatted with him. The door in the tower had materialised and Zami had glimpsed the strongbox within.

"Think the Filth'll come out?" Zami asked.

Afaq pointed to the dozen constables, who were trying to look casual, lining the steps of the imposing Georgian building that dominated the square. "They *are* out, making sure we don't break in, like."

"No, I mean an officer, someone in charge. To talk to us."

Afaq shrugged. "Dunno. Depends how clever they are, I suppose."

Zami was sure an officer would be out soon. Good community relations dictated that you talked to the mob before things got ugly. There were maybe fifty protestors, most of them young firebrands with proper beards, but including a smattering of older people – parents and neighbours.

The crowd grew restive in a slow, tidal undulation, and a chant swelled of "Release Abdul Bari! Release Fouad!" Zami added his voice. The coppers on the steps tensed, standing more erect. The dense black doors of the station remained closed. With no rhythm, the slogan was hard to maintain and died away.

Zami yelled, "Come on out. Talk to us. Tell us what's happening."

That had a more emphatic metre, and the crowd took up the chant, hammering out each syllable. "Talk To Us. Talk To Us."

Afaq shot Zami a smile and a respectful nod. With nothing much happening from the police, the two men moved to the back of the crowd where they could chat. At first it was religious – about *sharia*, according to Afaq, a superior system of law.

"It's Allah's law, not man's law, innit?" he said. "All the way back to the Prophet, peace be upon him, not something politicians can twist in their own interests."

Then Afaq began to talk about his information technology studies, and how he hoped to do as well as his brother.

"He's really clever, I mean really clever," Afaq said. "And strong."

Zami already knew all this, but the important thing was that Afaq was sharing with him, trusting him.

A handful of youths in hoodies emblazoned with the English Cross of St George tried to join the coppers protecting the station. The constables politely saw them on their way, and they sauntered off with shouts of "Muslim paedos."

Afaq shook his head. "Wankers."

After twenty minutes, a uniformed officer with braid on his cap pushed open the doors and positioned himself on the top step. Zami noted the crown on the man's epaulettes. A superintendent! They were taking this seriously!

"Where's Abdul Bari? Where's Fouad?" voices roared from the crowd.

The superintendent held up his hands for quiet and slowly a hush fell.

His voice was strong, carrying across the square. "We're still questioning the two Iqbal brothers. But there is no reason for alarm. This is all normal."

"That's a laugh. You kicked in the door," someone shouted, garnering mutters of agreement.

"We were acting on intelligence," the officer said. "Intelligence received from you, the community."

They must be rattled, Zami thought, if they were being this open.

"Yeah, right," someone at the front of the crowd yelled. Others laughed.

The superintendent's voice boomed across the cries. "We can't police without the consent of the community."

"Well you didn't have my consent to kick in Mrs. Iqbal's door, mate." That was Rashid, at the front.

Others took up Rashid's challenge, shouting, "Not mine either. Not mine."

"Frightened her half to death, didn't it?" Afaq advised Zami. "Poor lady."

The Superintendent waited, impassive, for the shouts to die away.

"I understand your concern," he resumed, "and I can tell you that Abdul Bari Iqbal will be released shortly without charge. We have applied for an extension of custody for Fouad Iqbal while we investigate further."

He paused again while the crowd digested this news, people discussing with each other in small knots. They churned like a boiling pot. Someone yelled, "You're fishing."

"Do they have anything on Fouad?" Zami asked Afaq.

Afaq pursed his lips. "Could be. On his Twitter, maybe."

Zami raised an eyebrow, inviting more confidences, but Afaq offered only an enigmatic smile.

"Release Fouad Iqbal." Rashid again. "Allah will judge Fouad, not Man."

An elder with a great white beard stepped in, and Zami saw the man remonstrate with Rashid, waving his hands and shaking his head.

"We depend on the community," the superintendent declared, raising his voice over the shouts from the crowd. His tone signalled he was winding up. "We can only keep you safe with your support."

"You're not," Rashid yelled. "The police attack us."

Again the elder sought to calm Rashid, making patting motions with his hands, but there were supporting growls from the younger men.

The constables bunched up on the step, protecting their commander. Some in the crowd edged forward. Just when it looked like things could get nasty, the cops produced their rabbit from the hat. The doors swung open to reveal a chubby young man, his boyish face hidden behind incongruous florid whiskers. The lad punched his fist in the air, to applause from the crowd, and the phalanx of constables opened to let him through to his supporters.

As he passed, the line of policemen sidled down the steps, chivvying the released boy away. Evidently, a brother in the hand was worth two in the cop shop, and many followed Abdul Bari as he allowed himself to be gently urged on his way. The demonstration fizzled.

Zami and Afaq joined the surge of protesters, eager to hear Abdul Bari's news.

"Weren't much," he declared. "Just, like, loads of questions about who I know and what they're into and stuff. They didn't break me. I gave them nothing."

"Did they question you about Fouad?" Rashid asked.

"Yeah, about who his friends are and what he does on the Internet. Like that."

"*Kufars*!" Rashid spat.

Zami added, "Bastards!"

Rashid glanced at him and smiled. "It's good you was there today, bruv. That was great, when you shouted them to come out."

Zami's return smile was grateful and studiedly without guile.

Yes, it had all been going so well until Rashid caught him and Ayesha in the park. Caught? That wasn't the right word – they hadn't been doing anything. And yet Zami felt like they had been discovered at something. Guilty conscience, perhaps? Carnal thoughts? Was Ayesha as chaste a Muslim woman as she appeared? She dressed modestly, to be sure, but her laughter had been free and earthy. Like her aroma. She smelled of the earth and knew about the stars.

Only in magical Granada, much later, did Zami learn whether Ayesha was indeed virgin or not. Granada, with the sun high over the Alhambra and the scalding siesta light spilling through the open window. Unable to wait until evening, they had reached feverishly for each other. Ayesha's cries mingled with those of a bird circling on thermals above the citadel.

Rejected by the brothers at midday prayers, Zami slouched from the mosque, hands shoved deep in his trouser pockets, shoes scuffing the pavement, feeling a mixture of dejection and elation. Ayesha had got in his way. Or was it Rashid who had got in his way? Which was his target? A pain ached his jaw, and he made the effort to unclench his teeth, relaxing his balled fists at the same time. This was not how it was supposed to go.

He reached the end of the street where Ayesha kept the family shop. He stopped. Cut down the street and she would be there, behind her counter, with obsidian eyes and a smile that lit the shadowed interior. Veer away towards the city centre and he might make his peace with Rashid if the brothers were manning the literature stall outside the mosque.

Zami turned away, following the road down to the train station. That was better. It would be safer for Ayesha.

But ill fate was not yet done with Zami. He heard steps at his shoulder, and half-turned. A bulky figure with that damn swaggering sailor's roll to his gait.

"Hello, Vince, me old mate. I've been looking for you," said Tommy.

CHAPTER 6

Does Tommy know about Ayesha?
Zami surprised himself with his first reaction – there was nothing to know, but he was sure Tommy wouldn't approve. Tommy probably didn't screw at all – not girls, boys, or sheep. Tommy had no weaknesses and never failed.

"Tommy, fuck off. You'll blow my cover," Zami said.

"Can't do that, Vince. I'm your handler, as of now." His smile was smug. The bastard intended that to wound him.

"You're in Special Branch now too? How did that happen?" Zami had transferred out of the Special Demonstration Squad to national security work with the Branch, largely to get away from Tommy.

"There ain't no SDS anymore. It was wound up, wasn't it? Still, we had fun there, didn't we, mate?"

Yeah, right, if Tommy's idea of fun was taking all the credit for his work. It was Zami who'd infiltrated the Speltborne Animal Rights loonies, he who'd uncovered the plan to blackmail the pharma companies, he who'd busted the raid on the animal testing laboratories. But it was Tommy, as the principal investigator, who'd got the commendation.

"Not here, for Chrissakes," said Zami.

"Tut, tut. Don't you mean for the Prophet's sake?" Tommy's grin broadened, wide enough to swallow the galaxy.

The thought of galaxies brought back Ayesha and stargazing in the park. If only he'd turned down the other street and popped into the shop, he would have avoided Tommy. But, he realised, not for long.

"Not here, somebody will see us. You'll blow my cover," Zami hissed in resignation. "I'll meet you at the station café in Brookhurst in an hour. Please, get the train after mine, not the same one."

"Fair enough, me old mucker. You take the train, I'll go by car. None of this would have been necessary, you know, if you'd checked-in like you're supposed to."

Zami wrapped his arms tight about himself, and then forced them to his sides again. *Two minutes in the bastard's company and already the score was 1–0 for Tommy!*

Foot raised and planted, followed by the other foot as he trudged the couple of blocks to the station. Lungs inflated and deflated. Blood circulated. All the mechanisms of his body worked, but his mind was a whirl. On the platform, sun beat down, and he retreated under the shade of the wooden awning.

His train pulled in, and he slumped in a seat. Other passengers pushed past, and he shifted over beside the window, looking at the carriages on the next platform.

A whistle blew. They seemed to move, but backwards, the carriages of the neighbouring train grumbling by. Zami felt no press of acceleration – he was suspended, motionless, while the world sped away from him.

Forward or backward, stationary or in motion, it was all a matter of frame of reference. Past and future coincided with the present – they were the same. A vortex inwards.

An old terror, leathery wings enfolding him in darkness – Malachi. Malachi was here. The paternal voice growled. "Come, boy, you've earned yourself a beating."

Tommy's mocking smile when he made sergeant before Vince.

And then a voice, warm and loving, a mother's voice, "Don't go out too far, you can't swim." She was here too, Ishtar.

Brighton shingle crunching beneath his toes, ice cream melting in the sun, deckchairs flapping in a sudden wind.

Dad, why couldn't you love me? What did I do that made you bring the murk? Malachi laughs. "You have your mother's weakness."

Washing, clean and white, fluttering in the little back garden. A scent of soap powder, and Malachi's wings withdraw, leaving sunlight's love, sharp as knives.

Vince's first encounter with cooking a green pepper, not knowing to cut the top off and core the seed mass, and the sense of elegance when he saw it demonstrated.

A love he was always scared of losing, a girl whose name he no longer remembered, who had urged a hefty rugby player to stand on her stomach to prove the strength of her abdominal muscles.

Giving evidence in the trial of the Speltborne Four.

A vortex outwards. Forward motion. Ayesha leaning back in his arms, her lips opening as he recited. The search through the Al-bayyazin for a fasting priest. A discussion with Rashid about who might be innocent. Water sparkling in the long canal of the Court of the Myrtles in Boabdil's palace. He wondered if this was really happening, or if it was a story he was telling himself.

Stories held a brutal, loveless world at bay, remade it heroically. King Arthur, Sinbad, and Odysseus all comforted him as a boy. Some tales were real, like the trip to Granada with Ayesha. Other were invented, but no less compelling for that. His favourites were the myths of the old Sumerian world, like the story of Gilgamesh. Those ancient legends held powerful truths – the young gods who fought and defeated the original pantheon of Mesopotamia; characters who were neither good nor bad; the location of the Garden from which the original man and woman were expelled. They told of flawed heroes and petulant deities, like Dad and Mum.

Shards of sunshine scatter from Ishtar's armour as she flies at Malachi, scarf veiling her face like an assassin. Though she had abandoned him as a child, she still protects him with a mother's ferocity. The world lurches as they tussle. Zami laces his fingers to form a star, symbol of Ishtar. Malachi snarls, tearing at Ishtar. And yet his tone is calm as he turns his great head to Zami. "Let it collapse, boy. Let it all go." Potential collapses into actuality. There is another lurch and a whistle, shrill and keen as a flight of arrows.

Then the train opposite cleared the platform, leaving it empty and stationary. Zami's frame of reference juddered and fell back into place. His carriage remained stationary.

Another whistle, and his train lurched into motion.

Tommy, always bloody Tommy!

There had been Tommies in his life as far back as he could remember. Always jeering, always right, always better.

He and Tommy went through Police Academy together, and both went undercover with the Special Demonstration Squad at the same time. And now the arsehole was here, muscling-in on his act. Again.

The train chugged through wooded countryside, followed by a lake and an estate of identical red-brick houses, before slowing, and pulling into Brookhurst station, dragging Zami back to the present.

Tommy was already seated in the café, nursing a tea. The small room was packed, making private conversation impossible. Zami shrugged. Tommy nodded imperceptibly and jerked his head. Zami followed him as he rose and left the station.

Twenty feet behind Tommy, Zami rounded the perimeter of the building and passed over a level crossing. An open cemetery stretched on the other side of the far platform, and he followed Tommy through the gates. He gave his handler time to disappear up a hill into a bushy area before again setting off in pursuit.

The din of traffic and the hubbub of voices hushed in the gentle stillness. The song of blackbirds and the irate alarm of a robin filled the air, and the breeze in the foliage muffled the conversations that rumbled through the earth from headstone to headstone.

Zami was well into the shrub cover now, an ideal spot for a quiet chat, but there was no sign of Tommy. He scanned the way back down the hill to see if he'd missed a forking path. Nothing. He moved on slowly upwards. He heard the rustle of branches behind him parting, and Tommy leapt out of concealment.

"Boo!"

"Don't be such a fucking idiot, Tommy. What are you? Thirteen?"

"Just checking on you, mate. You never were much cop at surveillance."

Zami feigned indifference.

"I'm not doing surveillance, am I? I'm undercover."

"So deep undercover you disappeared beneath the surface. That's why I had to come looking for you, you wanker. Can't you follow instructions at all? You were told to check in once a week."

Zami saw his opportunity and struck back.

"That would be clever, wouldn't it? Marching up to the cop shop to clock-in when there's demonstrations going on outside about the Iqbal brothers. Right!"

"You've got a phone," Tommy said, unfazed.

"And Rashid is an IT graduate," Zami replied.

"So?"

Zami sighed. "So I can't be sure my phone is secure."

"Then get a burner phone, you numpty."

"Yeah, I'll do that when I have time. Busy now."

Fingers stroking the morning's clean shave, each side of his face in turn, Tommy looked unconvinced. Zami mirrored the action, emphasising the fullness of his two-month growth.

"Okay," said Tommy, "so what have you got to report?"

"It's early days yet, but I think I'm getting Rashid and Afaq's trust."

Tommy fixed him with an unblinking stare and fished a cigarette from his pack, tapping it on the box. *Yeah right! No way was Tommy old enough to have smoked cigarettes where the tobacco needed to be packed down by tapping. It was a mannerism he'd picked up, imitating older coppers.*

At last he lit the cigarette and blew out a cloud of smoke. "And?"

"And nothing. It takes time. You know that, Tommy."

That seemed to satisfy him and he nodded, offering over his fag packet.

"No thanks," Zami said. "Tobacco and alcohol are *haram*, forbidden."

"Wow! You really do get into character don't you, Vince?"

Zami frowned, but did not correct the name. "I do my job well and professionally. Anything less would be failure. By the way, if you need something to go on, check Fouad Iqbal's Twitter account."

"Already done, me old mate, that's ancient news." Tommy looked cocky and waited.

Zami complied. "So what did you find?"

"A couple of retweets of some *jihadi* nonsense, but mainly fundraising for dodgy charities."

"And those idiots stirred up the whole community for some fundamentalist fundraising? Look, Tommy, if you're really supposed to be my handler, then handle it. Get the flatfeet off my pitch and let me dig in. Rashid will give me the good stuff if you let it simmer. He's starting to trust me." Zami added, "I think I can get close to him through his sister. She likes me."

His tale was starting to unfold, spread out ahead of him like a river delta viewed from the air. He needed luck, and the luck would buy him time.

As Zami paused to consider this, Tommy couldn't have known that he was breathing shallowly to conceal the commotion of his heartbeat. Tommy might have known there was a blackbird with one milky eye foraging through the underbrush near his feet. But, eyes fixed on the skyline, he didn't glance that way, and the bird, with its blind eye towards him, didn't see Tommy.

Zami noticed both – the unseeing man and the blind bird. He understood the bird as a sign, an element for a composition, a pointer to his future. The bird shuddered, like a moth in a cocoon, and distended into a crow. Zami moved with stealth, so as not to disturb the bird, until he was on its right hand side, facing the sightless eye, facing Tommy's right side. He just needed to keep on Tommy's blind side, tell him what he wanted to hear, and everything would be okay.

On the brow of the hill, the breeze stirred a tall beech sheltering a look-at-me funerary obelisk. Fists of foliage on either side of the main trunk punched the air in triumph. Refracted through the leaves, the sun's rays formed an eight-pointed star, Ishtar's sign. For Ishtar was not only the deity of love and war, but also of green fertility.

"We'll set up a drop box and I'll contact you when I have something, Tommy."

He considered the stone wall at the park entrance. There was a hole by the left pillar, where a stone had come out. But then a sudden and delicious thought occurred to Zami.

"Tell you what, the information will be in the doggy-doo waste bin in the park at midday if there's a report. For now, just stay out of my way. Don't ever follow me after mosque again. And if you want to make yourself useful, keep the local plod from trampling all over everything."

Tommy frowned, his mouth working, but before he could answer, Zami was off down the path calling a "you have a nice day now" over his shoulder.

Tommy yelled, "Oi! Where are you staying?"

"Need to know, Tommy mate. Need to know."

For once, he'd bested Tommy, and it felt good. When you won, you were worthy of love, of respect.

CHAPTER 7

Zami sat in his little room on the south side of the city, hunched over a notebook, a cup of coffee cooling and ignored on the table beside him. Rain pawed the closed window, but Zami didn't let it in. His thoughts were far away. He was busy crafting final detail for his legend.

The term "legend" wasn't approved police jargon, but he liked it better than cover. A cover was something you wore, while a legend you inhabited. And it populated you, making you stronger, faster, better.

He told himself all of us are the stories we tell ourselves and other people. And if they are believed, the legends become true.

Parents, early childhood – there was no reason to invent these. An absent mother, a distant and punishing father. Truth makes the best legends. He omitted the Hendon police college, of course. A misspent youth and a little dealing filled in those years. The figure that emerged from the shadows was bold and buccaneering.

Zami strode the deck of his vessel with a rolling gait, balanced against buffeting squalls. He reached to the table for his tot of grog. It was cold. He spat, too immersed to make a fresh cup.

And then, after the period of minor criminality, he sketched in revelation, conversion, redemption. What had brought him to Islam? A chance encounter? A deliberate search? Both had merits. Zami decided the deliberate search would be better – it allowed him political motivation. The Gulf war, a government that lied, a quest to understand. Maybe he had a friend who had served in Iraq? No. Then he'd have to invent the friend. Keep it simple.

Job? Well, that bit had already been built. Something vague, something in the creative industries, allowing him plenty of free time during the working day. Jobbing copywriter, if pushed. Or how would itinerant storyteller work? Perhaps a little too close to the truth. Freelance copywriter, it was.

A driving licence, bank cards, and other ID had already been issued. These he fleshed out with an online presence, turning to his laptop to create accounts for Twitter and Facebook and populating them with suitable posts. Zami scanned his notes, committing them to memory, then tore the page from his notebook and shredded it, sprinkling the pieces, in a snowfall of fiction, into the loo.

Legend inhabited, he squared his shoulders and stepped out to face the world.

On the bus journey into the centre of town, everything he saw was in its rightful place and he met them with an affable smile. The stallholders tended their pitches, the lovers giggled, the workers crossed between offices, and the tendency of everything was in line with expectation.

As he strolled towards the mosque, Zami became conscious of his swagger, a captain-ish roll to his gait.

He was the hero of his legend, and his legend was a fine thing.

Worshippers were gathering in the mosque precinct for the noon prayer. Zami slowed and mingled, a fish flickering in the stream. He spotted Rashid, eyes darting over the watercourse. Zami became a fisherman, straddle-legged and casting, a mariner playing a running marlin.

I cast my net and draw it in teeming. As the Lord says, let the creatures of the sea inform you.

Zami raised a hand and called, "Hello, Rashid, me old mate, *as salaam alaikum.*"

"*Wa alaikum as salaam*, brother Zami," Rashid replied, rolling towards him like a sailor. The unpleasantness in the park seemed to have been forgotten, or perhaps it was something he chose not to bring into the mosque.

The fish was hooked or the fish had hooked him.

Both men turned at a sudden commotion, close to the mosque gates. At first, all they could see was a wave of young men converging on the entrance, shouting. As Zami and Rashid ran closer, they saw the group confronting a gang of a dozen youths in hoodies emblazoned with the English Cross of St. George. Some gang members wielded large crucifixes.

"Time to fight ... Islamic terror," the youths chanted.

"Racist scum ... off our streets," one of the defenders hurled back with the same cadence, and the others took up his cry.

The youths' taunt changed. "Muslim paedos ... groom our children."

A bravo from the Muslim side danced out of their ranks, making V signs with both hands at his enemy. A beefy fascist scythed his crucifix through the air, and the bravo danced back, to cheers from his friends. The cross-bearer was pulled in by his mates. Both lines tremored and pulsed with energy. A distant siren wailed.

Rashid joined the Muslim line, greeted as a captain by his fellows. Zami stood just behind him, capering from foot to foot.

"Racist scum, off our streets," yelled Rashid.

"Off, off, off." The chorus jabbed their fingers at the intruders.

The two lines closed, pushing and elbowing, wavered, and separated again.

"Off, off, off," Zami yelled. The angry chant sang in his blood like the sea.

"Well look. A white Mooslim," crowed one of the gang.

"Traitor, traitor, traitor," his mates chorused.

The siren drew closer.

Zami knew that when the police arrived they would not distinguish between fascists and defenders. Tempers would fray, there would be arrests, perhaps heads would be broken if the riot squad had been scrambled. He plucked at Rashid's shoulder, trying to draw the man back. The shoulder shrugged him off.

An orange flew from the fascist line past Zami's face. He flinched. Behind him, a scream. Turning, he saw a cheek sliced open. Blood flowing red onto the white of a *shalwar kameez*. The fruit rolled on the ground, razor blades, embedded in its flesh.

The siren was a cry of anger. A screech of tyres. Blue lights. Two vanloads of police leapt into the fray, batons drawn, drumming on riot shields. The fascists broke and scattered.

"Get out of here," Zami yelled at Rashid, pulling him away. Through the crowd. Into the plaza.

The police had formed a line and were advancing slowly to the drumbeat of batons on plastic. The angry defenders retreated, step by step.

"Why you doing us?" one of them yelled. "It's the Nazis, innit?"

Another voice. "Police protect the fascists." And the crowd took up the chant.

Rashid tried to pull away from Zami, to get back to his fellows.

"Don't be stupid, Rashid," Zami hissed, still tugging. He couldn't afford for his target to be arrested.

The imam had come from the mosque, squeezing through the scrum and placing himself between the police and the crowd. "Calm, brothers, be calm. The trouble's over, it's done. No need for fighting. Peace, brothers."

The frail old man turned and faced the police. He was so small, Zami thought, and the black-clad cops in their body armour were so big. Body armour? Shields and batons? The station commander had over-reacted for sure. Probably because this involved Muslims. The advancing police line stopped. The imam stretched out his hands, empty palms towards the coppers. It might have been an act of surrender. Or it might have been the calming gesture of a tired parent to unruly children.

The crowd fell silent. Zami swallowed.

"No need for trouble, officers. No trouble." The imam's reedy voice rang soft and clear in the silence as the squad stopped drumming on their shields. "No trouble here."

And the tension blew away, spindrift on a beach. The attackers were long gone. The phalanx of youths, looking a little sheepish, allowed the imam to shepherd them towards the mosque. And the black-armoured curtain wall broke apart into individual men, joking and grumbling as they clambered back into their vans.

Zami walked with Rashid into the building, and they washed together. "That was pretty hairy, you get me?" Zami said.

"Yeah, we stood our ground and drove them off," said Rashid. Clearly he too was crafting a legend. "I cast my net and, lo, it's full of fish," he recited from the Qu'ran.

"How do you mean?"

"Well, it's obvious, innit? They attacked the mosque, and now the brothers will understand. It's us or the *kufars*."

CHAPTER 8

Ayesha came to him after the *Zuhr* prayer, full of shame. "Zami, I'm so sorry for Rashid's behaviour in the park. He is a man, but also a boy, pretending to be a man. Because our father is old, Rashid thinks he must lead the family, but he has his own family to look after. He should stick to that. It makes me so cross. Papa may be old, but Rashid's attitudes are like something from the Middle Ages. Can you forgive him please? And forgive me?"

Her gaze was bold and direct, but still she looked over her shoulder to check they weren't being watched. The precinct was still packed with worshippers. Zami saw her agitation and drew her gently into a side street, and then into a doorway. Her earthy scent was mingled with that of industrial cleansers blown on the breeze from the laundrette at the end of the alley.

"There's nothing to apologise for, sister, truly. Rashid was trying to protect you, that's it. I like him, respect him."

The rigidity of her shoulders relaxed a little. The ardour in her eyes was banked, and he saw gratitude.

"And I like you," he added.

She touched him. Softly, on the hand. The wind bowled a plastic bag along the lane, caught it, and swept it on an eddy into the sky. Aloft, it fluttered white wings, dipping and weaving. A bird called high and sweet. The back of Zami's hand tingled, the imprint of her fingers memorised by his nerves, though her touch had been fleeting.

She lowered her gaze but her voice was strong and vibrant. "Yes, I like you too. You didn't laugh at me when I talked about astronomy and stuff. Do you know how rare that is? For a man to treat you like a person?"

"Laugh? No, why would I laugh at you? It was interesting. None of my friends talk like that, and it made me imagine a world of possibilities."

There was laughter in the road. A boy and a girl walked past, holding hands. Zami and Ayesha moved to opposite sides of the doorway, but the young couple, rapt in each other's company, paid no attention. Zami realised he and Ayesha were invisible, if only they kept still. The blind, milky eye of strangers' stories protected theirs. All he need do was find Rashid's milky eye.

"Perhaps we could ..." Ayesha said. "No, it's silly."

"What?"

"Forget it. Nothing."

"Ayesha, you were going to suggest something. Whatever it was, I promise I won't mind. If that's what you were worried about."

She stared at the ground, then up at the sky. Her jaw worked but no words emerged. Zami smiled, nodded, encouraging her. At last she found her voice, eyes fixed on his.

"Okay, I was just thinking maybe we could talk again sometime. Somewhere Rashid couldn't spoil it."

"I'd love that, Ayesha." He had been planning to say "like", but it came out more enthusiastic than he'd intended.

"Where? When? I have the afternoon off on Wednesday."

He understood it would be improper to invite her to his tiny flat on the west side of town. "How about Brookhurst station café?"

She shook her head. "Too many people passing through, but Brookhurst's a good idea. Away from here."

"The cemetery alongside the station's quiet."

She laughed. "The grave's a fine and private place, but none, I think, do there embrace."

"Huh?"

"Andrew Marvel, *To His Coy Mistress.*"

Zami had no clue what she was talking about. But the words "embrace" and "mistress" formed ripples in his thoughts.

She seemed to sense his bewilderment. "English metaphysical poet. Seventeenth century."

"Ayesha, you astound me. Is there no end to the stuff you know? Andalusian astronomers and now English poets."

Her laugh was clear and sweet as a flute. "Poetry they say, is the record of the Arabs. It runs deep in Islamic culture." She recited once more. "As lines, so loves oblique may well themselves in every angle greet; but ours so truly parallel, though infinite, can never meet."

"Marvell again?"

"Yes. I can lend you a book of his poems if you like them."

"You shame my ignorance. I hardly know my own culture and yet you can quote from it."

"English literature is my heritage too. I'm British, born and raised." Her tone held the gentlest of reprimands.

"Of course, I'm sorry."

Ayesha smiled, and Zami noticed how white were her teeth, how easy her joy. He desired to taste that joy, to be the cause of it. A silence lengthened between them, but it was a comfortable, companionable thing.

Zami's awareness expanded. A radiance filled the narrow alley. The sun, shifting round the edge of a tower block, unleashed an eight-pointed torrent of light that boiled and bubbled down the arid gloom of the lane. A finger of luminosity stroked Ayesha's cheek, painting her skin a warm brown he longed to touch. His palm tingled with the imagined heat of her flesh. The light identified and transfigured her – she was meant to be his beacon. This was not the old Ayesha of the mouldy shop and the jealous brothers. No, this was Khawlah bint al-Azwar, the seventh century Arab Boadicea, leading the fearless charge by the Prophet's army on the Byzantine defenders at the siege of Damascus. Warrior Ayesha was as strong and funny and tender and bold as Ishtar.

He felt Khawlah would lead the charge for him. Keeping secrets from Rashid wasn't such a difficult thing. Ayesha was a tiny lie compared with his mission. She might even help the task. She provided his "in" to the quarry, just as he'd told Tommy. Rashid mistrusted him as a stranger, of unknown affiliation. But strangers are just comrades we haven't yet acknowledged. Rashid would grow to accept the liaison. And Ayesha wasn't a hindrance but a necessity – she would help him in his quest. She'd be able to find out things, make entries for him, smooth his path.

The quest to investigate Rashid and Afaq and the quest to hold Ayesha in his arms travelled the same road. They were one and the same. It was against regulations. But this went beyond convention. To win, the paladin had to follow his own path, make his own rules. Tommy mustn't know. Tommy was the enemy, as much as Rashid.

Zami chopped his arm through the air, warding off enemies. Without thinking, he laced his fingers into a star. Ayesha raised an eyebrow.

"How about we meet in the Costa?"

Which of them had suggested that, Zami could not afterwards remember. Perhaps they both voiced it at the same time, two stories animated by the same words.

"Two o'clock?"

"Perfect."

CHAPTER 9

Brighton shingle crunching beneath toes, ice cream melting in the sun, deckchairs flapping in a sudden wind – seaside holidays populated Zami's memories of childhood. Innocent, warm.

Here, today, this holiday was different – illicit, thrilling, after months of dodging and planning. Rain was driving hard against the lounge window when they reached Gatwick airport, baggage carts slaloming through the puddles on the tarmac. And then they were on the plane, in transition between the mundane and the imagined.

Ayesha took the window seat, her *abaya* wrapped tight around her, keeping up a nervous stream of chatter.

"I saw a town below," she said.

Zami leant across her to peer out at the landscape as she described it, smelling her scent of flowers with the underlying hint of loam. Her body was warm against him, and her dark eyes sparkled, framed by her best black hijab, trimmed in gold.

Neither of them mentioned Rashid and Afaq, but Zami's thoughts bustled with imaginings of what her brothers would do if they knew. From the family's point of view, it was shocking enough that Ayesha walked alone without a male chaperone.

"We're over Spain," Ayesha said.

"How can you tell?" Zami asked.

"I can't, I just sense it. I feel I'm coming home."

Moorish Spain, Andalusia, was Ayesha's spiritual home. She breathed the names of the great Kings and Andalusian scholars as if she had known them personally. Until Zami met her, he had never heard of any of these people.

"We're over Andalusia now," she said. "It makes me so proud to be a Muslim. We once ruled in Europe in a caliphate that was tolerant and cultured, in a sea of barbaric Christian kingdoms."

Zami thrilled to Ayesha's companionship here with him, on their way to Granada. Her family believed she was visiting relatives up north.

They were matched. He couldn't compete with her learning. But he could bring her to tears recounting tales of Don Vincent, the fifteenth century Catholic student who had converted to Islam to win the love of Ayesha. It was Ayesha's story. And Zami's story too, for he had been called Vince before reciting the words of conversion – *Ashadu an la ilaha illa Allah, wa ashadu Mohammad rasoolu Allah*.

Granada, on arrival, was every magic thing they had dreamed. The afternoon lay warm and lazy on the town. An adamant Mediterranean sun, the merciful shadow of winding cobbled alleys, breezes off the River Darro, and the jewel of the Alhambra palace brooding on its cliff. Granada, where he would at last lie with Ayesha. Their little stone apartment with its terracotta roof in the old quarter, the Al-bayyazin, might have housed Don Vincent.

Dumping their bags at the door, Zami threw back the shutters, and the sun licked his cheek.

"Let's go exploring," Ayesha said. "Let's eat tapas by the river, go to a bathhouse, visit the Alhambra, everything."

The entrance to the bedroom stopped them short. The one double bed offered a shocking promise. But it was her transformation that created the real shock. She entered the bathroom wearing hijab and enveloping *abaya*. Zami waited. The creature who emerged wore a wraparound floral skirt, her nipples visible against the white cotton tee-shirt. She was magnificent in her abandon.

He gaped. "Don't you feel undressed without your normal clothes?"

"My *abaya*? Those robes aren't my clothes," she laughed. "They're my biohazard suit."

Zami didn't understand and raised an eyebrow.

"Protects me from wandering hands and catcalls."

They made the palace and its gardens wait. The somnolent cafés, the lanes, and the bright esplanade danced attendance beyond their door.

"Don't hurt me," Ayesha said,

And Zami smiled and promised. Then they reached for each other feverishly, unable to delay until evening. The scalding siesta light spilling through the open casement, Ayesha's cries mingled with those of a bird circling on thermals above the citadel.

To lie with Ayesha was to lie with every woman who had ever existed. Islam teaches that to kill an innocent is to kill all of humanity. To love an innocent, then, must be to love all humanity. It was pure and magical. Zami inhabited Don Vincent, finally in the arms of his Ayesha. A thousand ghosts sighed in pleasure with them, and the air itself rolled warm and content, wrapping itself around the pair. Their doubts were stilled and there was all the time in the world. He was worthy of love.

Time was running out but, oh! Luck was his! The magic words were spoken – "Ashadu an la ilaha illa Allah, wa ashadu Mohammad rasoolu Allah" and his story changed. Ayesha consented to be his.

The Darro, beyond their window, gurgled in soothing liquid counterpoint to their coupling. Don Vincent took it slow for he was a skilful lover, patient and knowing, and she was a maiden. Fear, love, hope, expectation and then bliss – these and more he read in her eyes as he broke against her like the sea.

In the alley outside their window a trader's donkey brayed, and they both laughed. She liked it so much that there could be laughter and he liked her liking.

Don Vincent thanked God, thanked Allah or Yahweh, and all the secret names of the Almighty.

In the world beyond their bed, the armies of the Catholic Kings were closing on Granada while Boabdil dithered and fought with his uncle. Ayesha's brothers encouraged Don Vincent's suit, now he was Muslim, believing he might protect them when the Christian hordes arrived at the city gates. Don Vincent knew only that Ayesha was his virgin in paradise. He worshipped her with his body and with his hands and with his mouth until she tented her long legs and arched her back. She yielded a long shrill cry like a bird.

Ayesha giggled and hugged Zami, "Do we have to hang the bedsheet over the balcony to prove my lost virtue?"

As the sun dropped slowly towards the west, they explored the cobbled riverside. They satisfied their hunger with chunky *patatas bravas*, savoury *albondigas, gambas al ajillo* and fresh green salad, washed down for Zami with cold, cold beer, and for Ayesha with cola.

Zami stroked the perspiration on the outer skin of the glass against his forehead. "Alcohol is *haram*."

Ayesha smiled. "So is sex with a woman who is not your wife."

"Are we damned?"

"Totally."

The beer and the small, plentiful mouthfuls of the tapas were just right. They wanted to bite everything, smell everything, sip everything.

"You smell of damnation," she said.

Zami thought she might be offended if he told her she held, for him, the aroma of the honest earth. "So do you," he said and they both laughed as if it was the funniest thing in the world.

"Let's visit the Alhambra," she said. "Now. I need to stand there now. Please."

In their three days in Granada, they visited the Alhambra twice. Even ruined, even half a thousand years later, it was a spectacle. Outwardly, it made little show. But, inside, airy courts and fountains were as exquisite as Ayesha's body. Tranquil pools reflected the geometric precision of the towers. The gardens were laid out as an earthly paradise, a complex hydraulic system lifting the Darro's waters against gravity to the top of the hill.

"How did they do that?" Zami marvelled.

"They were scholars," Ayesha said. "And artists."

"If we could only find Don Vincent's treasure tower," Zami said, "we could stay here for ever, guarding the secret and the riches, appearing only once every century."

When they saw the scar that Christendom had inflicted on the Alhambra after the conquest, Zami understood

Rashid's anger. Built diagonally across the complex, the palace of Charles V was an ugly monstrosity, two brutish fingers up to the elegance and delicacy of Boabdil's palace.

Zami wondered whether Rashid and Afaq were planning their own two-fingers-up to Western civilisation.

With time running out on the last day of their escape, the couple hired a car and drove towards the Sierra Nevada. They sought the spot where the defeated Boabdil turned, looked back at his lost city and sighed. Still known as the *Suspiro del Moro*, the Moor's Sigh, they, like other tourists, felt drawn to the mountain pass, nearly nine hundred metres above sea level, They too looked back at Granada, their arms around each other.

"You do well to weep like a woman for what you failed to defend as a man." Ayesha, a catch in her voice, quoted Boabdil's mother.

"What else could he have done?" Zami asked. "If he had fought, he would have been crushed. Moorish rule was finished in Spain."

"Our time too is ending here. Take me back to our house. Make love to me."

While Granada slept, every siesta time, the couple made sweaty, luxurious, forbidden love.

"Our souls are here," Ayesha decided. "With Don Vincent and Ayesha, with Boabdil and *Al Andalus*."

As they lay together in the tangled sheets, Zami was certain it would be easy and free from now on.

CHAPTER 10

Even before Granada Zami was gripped by the clandestine promise he had shared with Ayesha in the shop doorway. All lovers, he thought, should be secret. And then he smiled, knowing he was being premature – they were not yet lovers. But the pledge hung in the air. He had breathed in molecules of her scent and made them his own; her soft touch had fired the nerves on his hands. Already, his flesh carried an imprint of her.

One day, he would cup her breast while she lay in his embrace and instructed him in Moorish alchemy. And he would tell her tales while she quivered with anticipation. Zami was good at tales.

A promise links the future and the present, remakes the colour and texture of today with what is to come, he thought. It changes the direction of the story.

New hope coloured everything. Even Rashid, at prayers in the mosque, began to nod and then smile. Perhaps he felt that Zami's friendship with his sister could be a protection, rather than a threat. Zami warmed to the overture and resolved to be even more scrupulous in his behaviour towards her in Rashid's presence. It shouldn't be hard to win the brothers round.

Zami was contrite, he was sincere, he was persuasive. After mosque, he circled into Rashid's path, standing at an angle, not face on, letting his shoulders slump and his gaze drop.

"About the other evening, brother, I'm sorry. Really, I meant no harm. We were only talking about astronomy, Muslim astronomy. Your sister is so knowledgeable."

Rashid folded his arms. "My sister needs to know her Qur'an as well as she knows *kufar* science, you get me?"

"Women are always in need of guidance and protection, brother," Zami agreed. "The way you protected her, that was impressive. I would never disrespect her or your family."

That seemed to mollify Rashid, who smiled and uncrossed his arms, stroking his beard. Zami copied the gesture. Rashid's smile relaxed, and Zami smiled too. When you mirror someone's actions, it builds trust.

Afaq provided the break.

He caught up with his brother, looking even more contrite than Zami had. "I can't do Friday. Really sorry, bruv. I got a thing."

"A thing? What thing? What does that even mean? Where you think I'm going to get someone else to do the stall now with only a few days' notice?"

"I could do it," Zami offered. "Be pleased to."

"Wow! Thanks, brother." Afaq beamed at his saviour.

Rashid looked unsure. Afaq pressed his advantage. "It'd be good to have a white Muslim doing the *dawah*, yeah? Might even get up some interest from the Brits."

"All right, mate, thanks." Rashid extended a grudging hand and Zami grasped it, his grip firm but calibrated, making sure it was no stronger than Rashid's.

***

"Time is running out," Zami called to a passer-by. "Your Lord is most knowing of who has strayed from His way, and He is most knowing of who is rightly guided. Allah has a plan for us."

He brandished a pamphlet. But his thoughts were elsewhere.

Wednesday, he meditated, *only five days away. Ayesha's day off.*

A handful of Muslim youths browsed the stall.

"You remembered," Rashid said. "About Allah's plan, the draft plan and the final plan, innit?"

Zami wasn't sure where he had got the phrase about the plan, but then he recalled his first conversation with Rashid about the imam's sermon.

"Yeah," he said. "You helped me understand that."

"And you bought a book about the *Khilafah*. Did you read it yet?"

He had thumbed through it. "Yeah."

"And?"

"And it made a lot of sense. To live by the book, to keep Allah's law. That's better than what we got now, politicians lining their pockets and shitting on us."

"Not just doing us over. They make war on the *Ummah*, too," Rashid prompted.

"That too, yeah."

A full beard jerked up from his perusal of the pamphlets and fixed Zami with a stare. His eyes were a startling blue. "It's important, brother. Gassing and bombing our brothers and sisters in *Sham*. To hurt any member of the *Ummah* is to hurt all Islam."

It sounded like a speech the man had learned by rote.

"You'll get no argument from me," Zami said. And it was true. The carnage in Syria horrified him, the barrel bombs that rained down on Aleppo. No wonder brothers took up arms against the regime.

"And Iraq, and Afghanistan," Rashid added. "That *kufar*, Blair."

And Kosovo, Zami thought, but that doesn't fit the narrative – saving Muslims from Christian atrocities.

"It ain't no crime to want it. Muslims need our own State to protect us," the full beard was saying.

Rashid's lips tightened and his shoulders squared. This was dangerous ground, Zami knew, getting close to breaking anti-terrorist law. He saw calculation in Rashid's eyes and understood Ayesha's brother feared provocation, a set-up. The beard was no-one Zami had ever seen and didn't look like a plod. But you couldn't tell – he might be Intelligence.

Evidently, he wasn't anyone Rashid knew either and his reply was a non-committal "*Inshallah*." God willing.

The beard looked disappointed and drifted away.

"I don't know what to think of ISIS," Zami risked. "You hear bad things, but then they talk crap about Muslims all the time."

"You don't wanna believe everything they say," Rashid said.

"Tell me about it! But how do you find out what's true?"

Again Zami saw that tightening of the lips again, and that calculation. Rashid examined him. Zami smiled.

Rashid decided. "You wanna join our *usrah*, our study group, bruv, that's what you wanna do. Then you'll learn what's true."

He was in! He took pains to make sure none of the triumph reached his face. The face, he painted with mild pleasure. "Thanks, brother. I'd like that. When? Where?"

"Next Wednesday."

Fuck! Not Wednesday! Wednesday was for Ayesha.

"Wednesday evening after the *Isha* prayer, in the Ummah Centre."

Evening! Yes. Ayesha was the afternoon.

***

After they packed up the literature table, Zami went home and scribbled a note to Tommy, *Got into Rashid's study group*, and folded it into a plastic bag. At midday the next day he left the bag in the doggy-doo bin drop, relishing the idea of Tommy rooting through the rubbish. *Now let the bastard complain about lack of progress!*

CHAPTER 11

"This study group, this *usrah*. Do you know what *usrah* means literally, brothers? It means family, don't it? And today we're welcoming a new member to our family, brother Zami." Rashid extended a hand towards Zami, with a gesture that reminded him of an Old Testament prophet in a Cecil B de Mille film.

Rashid was the leader, of course. Round the table in the centre of the community meeting room sat six other men, all in their twenties or early thirties. Afaq he already knew, and Zami remembered two others from the demonstration outside the police station – they had shouted with particular zeal. He also recognised Abdul Bari, one of the two brothers the cops had detained. The stranger with the pinched features was possibly Fouad, the other brother.

Zami smiled. "*Alhamdulillah,* praise be to God, thank you for allowing me into your family."

The other men rose and shook his hand solemnly. Afaq clasped his forearm and smiled while pumping his hand. The nervousness Zami had felt when he woke that morning vanished. Now he was onstage, sure in his part.

After *Fajr*, the dawn prayer, Zami had struggled to swallow his breakfast of coffee and muesli. The cereal scratched like sawdust in his dry throat. Though he'd read up on Islam, he remained terrified of being caught out by the study group, his ignorance and errors on display.

Ayesha had shown him the way out. She was his hawk, the raptor who led him to his prey.

"Allah loves the ignorant," she had said as they nursed their coffees that afternoon. Both had chosen macchiato, and the coincidence had made them smile. They sat facing each other across the table as friends do. By the window, a sofa offered the possibility of sitting side-by-side like lovers. As they carried their drinks from the counter, they had looked at the sofa. And then at each other, before heading to the table. It was too soon for the sofa.

"If Allah loves the ignorant, he must really hate you," Zami said, with a wink. "You've learned so much about so many things."

A momentary sadness veiled her eyes before she laughed. "Perhaps he does. Truly, it's hard to find evidence to distinguish between the propositions 'God loves his children' and 'God hates his children'."

Zami wanted to reach out and smooth away the sorrow, but the boldness of her heresy thrilled him. She seemed to sense the tussle between sympathy and admiration in his heart, and a moment of sounding silence opened between them. Empires might have risen and fallen during the age in which they interrogated each other's souls.

"You're like nobody I've ever met," he said at last. "Why did you say that thing about ignorance?"

Her laugh was merry. "Why, because the ignorant have so much to learn. And nothing delights Allah more than learning. The Prophet, peace be upon him, said an hour's contemplation is better than a year's worship."

And that was all that Zami had needed. His dread about the study group vanished. He didn't have to be knowledgeable. All he needed was ignorance. Let Rashid be clever. Zami's lack of learning would flatter the man.

And so it proved later in the group. "Brother Zami," Rashid was saying, "we've been discussing how Allah wants us to live. That's our topic, how to live as good Muslims."

That seemed a tad disappointing. Zami had hoped they might have been planning holy war, *jihad*. Perhaps that was too much to hope for. Or perhaps this group wasn't really the cell.

"What do you think, brother?" Rashid asked him.

"I'm here to learn," Zami replied with an easy smile. "I don't yet understand enough to teach."

"Yes, but you must have an idea," Afaq said. "Everyone's ideas are welcome here. We're a band of brothers."

Did the phrase "band of brothers" mean a military purpose, or was it just an accidental expression? Did it invite him to raise the question of jihad? No, better to keep his persona simple, listen and learn.

"Well, this might be too naive, but as I've learned it, keep the five pillars of Islam." Zami counted them off on his fingers. "Testify to your faith. Observe the daily prayers. Fast during Ramadan. Pay your alms. Make the *haj* to Mecca."

Rashid observed him in silence, then watched the group, inviting comment. Afaq grasped the baton.

"Yeah, good, brother Zami, but is that enough? Not really. We gotta read the Qu'ran too."

Zami worried this might be a test. "Sorry, yes, of course."

"You need to understand Islam direct, from the source. For yourself, innit?" Rashid said. "Not what men have written, but what Allah has written. Then there's what you owe others, your *fard al-kifaya*. When the community is weak, a Muslim steps in to strengthen it."

Now this was more interesting. "How do you mean, exactly?"

"You did the *dawah* stall, di'nt you? That was *fard al-kifaya*, community service. So is coming here to the group."

"Yeah, I get it." Zami beamed his face, his open smile portraying understanding and gratitude.

"And you stood up for Muslims, stood up for me and Fouad at the demo," said Abdul Bari. "That was *fard al-kifaya* too."

"I see, yes. Wow!" Zami's expression lay guileless, inviting elaboration.

Neither of the men from the demo had said anything yet, so he fixed one with an enquiring gaze.

"Standing up for the *Ummah*. Yeah, that's a duty," the man agreed.

"Muslims don't have no country," Afaq said. "It's better than that. We got the *Ummah*, the worldwide community of Muslims. Don't matter if you're from Britain, or from Saudi, or from Bangladesh, or from Sham. We're all one family."

Zami knew Sham meant the territory encompassing Syria and the Levant. In his mind he began drafting his report.

"That's right, brothers. That reminds me of this poem I found online," Rashid said. "I wanted to share it with you tonight. It expresses what the *Ummah* means."

Rashid liked poetry? Ayesha, yes. But Rashid?

Rashid recited from memory, his head thrown back and his voice deep and resonant.

*"My homeland is the land of truth,
the sons of Islam are my brothers.
I do not love the Arab of the South
any more than the Arab of the North.
My brother in India, you are my brother,
as are you, my brothers in the Balkans."*

There was more, a list of places, but Zami lost the thread of it. He watched Rashid's beard quiver as he declaimed, adding metre and rhythm to the words, like a cappella. Rashid sang with pride and longing as generations of Bedouin bards had around their campfires. Almost, Zami saw a burnous enfold the man, and fierce cold stars burn in the desert night.

Ayesha had been right when she said poetry was the soul of Islam.

When Rashid finished, the moment was filled with the awkward silence that happens when men share emotion.

Fouad broke the quiet. "That's great. I liked the bit about 'we are all one body, this is our happy creed'. Who wrote it?"

"Ahlam al-Nasr."

There were sage nods of approval. The name meant nothing to Zami, though he recognised it was female, and was surprised these bearded men should so appreciate a woman's writing.

"To Allah we belong and to him we will return," intoned Afaq. Perhaps Ahlam al-Nasr was dead.

"If only all Muslims thought like Ahlam," said Fouad.

"*Alhamdulillah*," Rashid agreed piously.

"Seems to me," Fouad said, "to be a good Muslim, you gotta fight for us to live by the *sharia*, you get me? So that one day all men can know the truth and live in Allah's mercy."

"And so what's stopping us?" asked Rashid.

Fouad had no doubt. "The armies of *Shaitan*."

"And our own darkness," Afaq added.

"That's right, brother," Rashid said. "Yeah, our own darkness. *Jahiliyya*, absolute ignorance, that's what Sayyid Qutb called it. Muslims have fallen into ignorance and lost their way. The powerful don't give up their power so easy. No, brothers, they trick us and they corrupt us, so we lose the rightly-guided path. We gotta get back to the truth."

Feet planted apart, Rashid looked up at the ceiling and again became the narrator at the campfire. "This one is by the Saudi, Isa Sa'd Al Awshan," he said, and the group nodded.

> *"The age of submission to the unbeliever is over,*
> *He who gives us bitter cups to drink.*
> *In this time of untruthfulness, let me say:*
> *I do not desire money, nor a life of ease,*
> *But rather the forgiveness of Allah and His grace.*
> *For it is Allah I fear, not a gang of criminals."*

Rashid explained that next week, they would begin reading *Social Justice in Islam* by Sayyid Qutb, and passed out copies.

Muslim Brotherhood – Zami found the connection in memories from his briefings. Qutb was the intellectual founder of the Muslim Brotherhood. He had something to report. And more than something.

The crucial piece of intelligence came not from the group but from Ayesha in the coffee bar. They had been talking about travel. Ayesha had explained how much she'd love to visit Andalucía in Spain, Al Andalus. Then, quite casually, she had mentioned that her brothers' travelled.

"They'd never want to visit Al Andalus," she'd said. "But they go off on trips around the country at the weekend."

Now that was interesting. Where were the brothers going? Ayesha hadn't known. Who were they meeting? What were they doing? Might they be attending weapons training camps? Or checking-out targets? What was the real nature of the study group?

As the group discussed details, Zami's mind drifted, captivated still by the echoes of Rashid's rendition of the poems. He didn't understand poetry but was in awe of it. How could a man love both poetry and killing, beauty and mayhem? Zami considered precedents. The Icelanders of old did that, didn't they, butchering their neighbours and then making up odes over the corpses?

And how could Rashid and Ayesha be born of the same mother? United by sharp minds and a delight in verse, Rashid was stern in righteous condemnation while his sister revelled in tolerance and enquiry. Ayesha was the twenty-first century face of Islam, and her brother its implacable medieval essence. And yet, Zami was coming to like them both immensely.

Leaving the community centre, Zami clapped Rashid on the back. Across the street, the coal of a cigarette glowed in the shadow of a doorway. A lad in a hoodie with the cross of St George on the chest cupped his hands around the flame of lighter, face like a Manga character in the stark shine. His mate with the lit cigarette stepped forward to take the lighter, looked at the *usrah*, and spat on the pavement.

CHAPTER 12

Zami, cross-legged on the carpet of Rashid's little terraced house, tore a piece of *naan* bread and mopped the last juices of *rogan josh*.

"You have a good appetite, brother Zami." Rashid's wife beamed and seemed pleased their visitor had found her hospitality good.

"How could I not? You are an excellent cook, sister Zainab."

Rashid turned to cuddle his son, but not before Zami had spotted the look of pride.

"More?" Zainab offered.

The scents of the spiced food were tempting, but he was comfortably full. If he refused, would she think he didn't really like the food? If he said yes, would she think she hadn't provided enough? Rules of hospitality were so complex.

Ayesha shot Zami a glance, as if sensing his dilemma, and pushed her empty plate away.

He smiled and did the same. "I couldn't manage another mouthful, thank you, sister."

"So you'll have no room for any mango *barfi*?" Zainab was teasing him, and he was pleased she felt comfortable enough to do that.

He felt his stomach and grinned. "There might be a tiny corner."

Zami looked again at Rashid, to check the mutual teasing broke no rules. With a smile, Rashid reached to the plate of sticky sweets and popped one into Zami's mouth. At first, he was shocked by the intimacy, but reasoned it must be a custom with guests.

Afaq laughed and also grabbed a *barfi*. Zami feigned protest as Rashid's brother also threatened to force-feed him. He would have liked Ayesha's fingers against his lips, but that could never happen in front of her family. Instead, Ayesha helped her sister-in-law clear the plates from the carpet and carry them into the kitchen.

The space was cleared just in time as Afaq rolled Zami onto his back, crossed legs helpless in the air, and tried to push another sweet into his mouth. Rashid's little son jumped astride Zami's chest, giggling and shouting, "Eat."

Ayesha clapped her hands like a mother. "Boys, boys."

Afaq frowned and then laughed. Rashid rose from the carpet, and stretched out on an over-stuffed red plush sofa, his fingers laced behind his head. Afaq offered a hand, helping Zami upright. The operation, with Zami's legs still crossed, was like righting a Humpty Dumpty. At last, Zami unscrambled the pretzel of his limbs, massaging aching thighs.

Rashid saw his discomfort and motioned him to an armchair. "You're not used to eating on the floor, are you, brother?"

And it was true, he wasn't, except for picnics. Lunching that way had been exotic, almost something forbidden. He felt he'd been let in, walked through a secret door into Rashid and Afaq's inner lives. Though he'd tasted the food on the table, the treasure hadn't vanished.

And it hadn't taken any spells to enter the tower. One day Rashid had just said, "You don't know nobody here, do you, brother? Have lunch with us after Friday prayers." Simple as that. He hadn't needed a fasting priest. But, of course, he did have the interest of a chaste maiden. Ayesha must have put in a good word.

Zainab cleared the last dishes away and Rashid fetched a *nargileh*, a hookah or hubble bubble as Zami called them. There were four hoses, though neither Ayesha not Zainab joined in. From somewhere unseen, Zainab produced a hot coal held in small tongs, dropping it onto the bowl of tobacco. Rashid put the mouthpiece to his lips and drew smoke through the bubbling rose-infused water, exhaling a contented cloud of smoke. Zami drew in a mouthful of fragrant tobacco. *Alhamdillulah*, he wouldn't need to find an excuse to slip into the garden for a crafty cigarette after all.

He expected Zainab and Ayesha to leave the men at that point. In fact, he'd been surprised the women had eaten with them at all. Perhaps Rashid wasn't as strict a conservative as Zami had believed. Stranger still, Rashid tolerated his sister engaging him in theological discussion.

The topic came up accidentally in a conversation about movies, and the lack of good Islamic stories. Afaq said he'd like to see a film about *jihad*.

Ayesha said, "You understand what *jihad* means?"

"Course I do," Afaq answered.

Rashid rolled his eyes. "Don't get her started, bruv."

Ayesha stiffened, her eyes flashing. "Okay, Afaq, what does *jihad* mean?"

"Holy war, innit?"

"No brother, sorry, it isn't. *Jihad* means struggle," she said.

"That's what I said."

"There's lots of kinds of struggle. When you study, you struggle with your ignorance. That's *jihad*. The Prophet, peace be upon him, spent more time in study than he did in war. To seek knowledge is a duty for all Muslims. When you work to make the community better that's *jihad*, too."

Afaq looked at Rashid, who smiled indulgently and said, "You're mixing up *jihad* and *fard al-kifaya,* holy war and community service."

"So you say, but is it not written in the Qur'an, 'Read in the name of your Lord Who created. He created man from a clot. Read and your Lord is the Most Honourable. Who taught by the pen. Taught man what he knew not.' Is it not a shame on Islam that in some of our countries illiteracy is twenty or thirty percent? And even more for women?"

Afaq, who had begun to pace the room, seized his opportunity. "Teach a woman to read and they can't tell the difference between *jihad* and *fard al-kifaya.*"

Ayesha's reply was cool and instant. "Teach a woman to read and she will teach her children. Teach a man and he'll swallow any old rubbish."

Afaq came to a halt behind her. He put his arms around her, holding her tight by the waist. Zami became aware of the space between his own arms, an electric space discharging sparks of possibility, and pressed his arms to his sides to extinguish the vacancy. Ayesha turned her head to look at her brother and laughed, warm and easy.

"You've run out of argument, haven't you?" she teased.

Still holding her pinned with one arm, he circled his other across her throat. Zami laughed, though he wasn't sure why.

"Islam don't need no arguments of man," Afaq said. "It's just true, whatever you think."

He strengthened his hold on her neck. "And nothing good awaits those who ignore Allah's teaching," he added.

Her voice emerged choked from the grip. "Violence is the last resort of the incompetent."

His features contorted, ugly for a moment. The sinews stood out on his arm as he squeezed.

"You're hurting, Afaq. Stop it," she cried.

Zami laughed again, but an uncertain mirth, awkward and manufactured. Perhaps this was a game the siblings played. But he itched to intervene, and glanced at Rashid, to find the man watching with cool interest.

"I will if you give up. Submit?" Afaq asked.

"Islam means submission to Allah alone," Ayesha gasped, her face flushing.

He frowned. "Don't be scared, sister. I'd never hurt you."

When he relaxed the choke hold, she coughed and, after she'd caught her breath again, she answered, "*There's no art to find the mind's construction in the face. You are a gentleman on whom I built an absolute trust.*"

The face she turned to Afaq was innocent and open, her smile easy and loving. Zami admired her cunning. There had been no need to protect her, his Khawla bint al-Aswar— she could take care of herself.

"What's that?" Afaq asked. "One of your quotes?"

Her eyebrows knit as she nodded. "Shakespeare."

"Yeah, families have absolute trust in each other. Total," he agreed.

Rashid reached his hand out, touching his brother's arm and giving a nod of his head.

"What do you say, brother Zami?" Rashid asked.

Zami smiled. "I know better than to interfere in family quarrels, you get me brother Rashid?"

Rashid laughed and Afaq inspected his feet. Ayesha held Zami's gaze, her face unreadable.

"Allah loves the ignorant," Zami said to her, "for they have so much to learn."

Now Ayesha laughed too, though only she and Zami understood what she was laughing at. Afaq seemed disconcerted, perhaps wondering if he'd just been called ignorant.

"Time for football," Rashid said, dispelling any remaining tension. Zainab exhaled loudly.

Zami patted his stomach. "Football? I couldn't, not after such a wonderful meal."

"No, I didn't mean playing. I coach the under-thirteens. Come and watch if you want."

Rashid kissed his wife and his son as if he were off on adventure. Then the three men strolled through the town to the park.

"Ayesha is too good for this world," Rashid said.

"Ayesha is too bossy for this world." Afaq was still stung.

"The idea of war is hard for women," Zami said, referring back to the discussion of jihad that had started the argument.

"War is hard for men too," said Rashid. "To go to war, you have to love humanity more than you love your wife and children."

Zami nodded. "And then you have to kill some of them."

"Killing wouldn't be so difficult," Rashid said. "Not to destroy Shaitan's soldiers."

Zami decided to probe. "Yes, *mano a mano* with another man. If it was war. But women and children die too."

Rashid stopped mid-stride, and Afaq, who had trailed behind almost ran into him. The elder brother gripped Zami's arm with a strange intensity.

"Yes," he said, "innocents die too. And, brother Zami, that worries me. It worries me so much. It is *haram*, forbidden. The Qur'an says if you kill an innocent, it's the same as killing all humanity, like."

"Then is war a sin?" Afaq asked.

"Maybe, I don't know."

Which was better? To catch Rashid or to save him?

Zami said, "I've got the same problem. I can see slaying people in a war, yeah. If they come at you, that's easy. But bombing a train, or a concert. How can that be right?"

Afaq listened intently, his gaze shifting from Zami to Rashid as they debated.

"But there is a war," Rashid said. "A war between Islam and the *kufar*, you get me?" He numbered them off on his fingers. "Palestine, Afghanistan, Iraq, Libya, Al Sham."

"Yeah, I get that, but does that make it okay to slaughter innocents?" Zami said.

"How many innocents do they massacre with their bombs and their drones? They brought it on themselves. Now let them weep."

"Those are governments, not the people."

"They still voted for the governments that dropped the bombs. And all the other wars. The war was wrong, the government was wrong, and the voters were wrong. The Qur'an says it is allowed to kill to save a soul, or when the soul you take is corrupted. The voters have blood on their hands too."

"Not all of them. Almost two million people in this country marched against the Iraq war. Are they guilty too?"

"Yeah. They elected the governments that support the Zionists and attack the Muslims."

"Okay, I'm with you on Israel. But what confuses me, is that Blair's government not only attacked Iraq, it went into Bosnia and Kosovo and stopped the Serbs massacring Muslims."

Rashid just stared at Zami, his face a mask.

Stupid, stupid, stupid.

"You believe they did that for the Muslims?" he asked at last. "Did Cameron and Obama stop the slaughter in Syria?"

"No, I guess not. You're right, Rashid."

The hardness eased from Rashid's face. They had shared something. Despite the hiccup, Rashid had let Zami see his doubt. He threw his arm around Zami's shoulder as they reached the park and the waiting lads.

CHAPTER 13

Call it guilty conscience, call it the need to share truth. But Zami's tales for Ayesha began to fold back on themselves until the line between worlds was worn paper-thin.

As the day's heat began to leech from the darkling sky, Don Vincent hurried back through the alleys of the Albayyazin to Ayesha. The purse, heavy with coin, tugged at his belt. Trade had been brisk today. His songs had captivated the crowd, and the audience had been generous. They had roared with ribald merriment at his bawdy ballads and silently wiped tears from their eyes at the lays of lost loves.

"Hoy, Don Vincent," a voice called. "Luck is running out. A bottle of luck for only one glass of time."

It was the Jew, Sandor.

Don Vincent stopped, cross-gartered legs apart, hands on hips, and offered a rumbling belly laugh. "Not mine, *amigo*. I have plenty of luck. Is business so bad you must accost the fortunate of the town?"

"Sadly yes, *señor*. Nobody has the time for luck these days. I barely eke out a living."

Don Vincent exhaled a stage sigh. "Had we but world enough and time." Then he brightened. "Let us roll all our strength and all our sweetness up into one ball and tear our pleasures with rough strife through the iron gates of life. Thus, though we cannot make our sun stand still, yet we will make him run."

"What?"

"Make time run fast, my friend. That's the secret."

"If you say so."

Don Vincent bade the young merchant of luck adios, knowing Ayesha would be back already from the Alhambra palace. He hurried, like time through the iron gates of life, to his wife and the rooms they shared on the banks of the Darro. Pausing at another stall to buy a plump capon, he opened his full purse with a flourish.

"Time is running out, *señor*," called old Adil, as Don Vincent strode past with the bird under his arm.

"Not for me, amigo. I have all the time in the world."

***

As Ayesha plucked the bird, Don Vincent plucked his lute, the notes rising into the jasmine-scented dusk. His playing was immaculate, his voice strong and merry, and Ayesha was captivated.

Though he sang often for the patrons in the plazas and squares, he performed for money. At home, he sang for the pleasure of her smile, and she repaid him in the coin of love.

"Tell me a story, *habibi*," she pleaded. "I live for your stories."

"We inhabit a wondrous story of our own making, *habibti*," he said, "a song of our own composing. We are the story, we are the song. There is no song separate from the singer, only a singing. We are the music of the spheres."

She completed the preparation of the bird, washed her hands, and snuggled against him, cool palm stroking his whiskered cheek. "A story, please."

"Oh very well, mi amor. You are as insatiable for tales as you are for love. I will tell you of how Zami tried to storm the citadel."

"Your stories transport me. Which citadel?"

"A maiden's citadel. Her name, like yours, is Ayesha."

"Time and again you tried to storm my citadel," she giggled, "but my walls were strong and did not crumble."

"Hush, *habibti*, who is telling the tale?" And Don Vincent began his narrative.

Zami wasn't his real name, his original name. At first he was called Vince.

"Like you, habibi. It's you!"

"Wait and see. If you interrupt, I'll never get to the end and you'll never know."

Ayesha set the capon on the trivets to roast over the fire and listened as she peeled carrots.

Zami came to the great city in search of fame and fortune. He was clever, blending in. People took to his easy manner and his warm smile. Nobody could spin a yarn like Zami, and he held listeners spellbound.

"It's you. It is."

Don Vincent held up a warning finger, and Ayesha, returned to the carrots.

One day, a courtier arrived at his door. The man was richly dressed in fine cloth, dyed kermes red, and a jewel in his turban.

"The Caliph has learned of your prowess as a storyteller," he said in a haughty tone, *"and summons you to the palace to recite for him."*

"Thank you, my man," said Zami. "I will come by and by."

"His Magnificence commands you now."

Now, Zami had heard the Caliph's fortress possessed a secret tower, guarded by a ghost, and that the tower held all manner of riches. He determined to make off with the crown jewels for his secret master, the sultan of a neighbouring state. So, of course, he was eager to enter the palace, but he feigned weariness and allowed the aide to cajole him, agreeing at last with a show of reluctance.

"Well, if you insist," he said. "But the guild of glassblowers will be most displeased. I was to perform for them this evening at the guildhall."

The courtier assured him that the glassblowers would be compensated, and the pair set off for the palace.

In the throne room, the Caliph received Zami with great courtesy, according him the status of a visiting ambassador.

"For, are you not an emissary from the kingdom of dreams?" said His Magnificence.

"That I am, Sire," the loremaster replied without a shred of false modesty, and the assembled courtiers gave a sigh of delight, as if he had promised them the choicest sweetmeats.

But the maiden at the Caliph's side snared Zami's gaze. She glanced at Zami and there was a fire in her eye before she looked down demurely. Ayesha, chaste and comely sister to the Caliph.

"You wicked liar," Ayesha said to Don Vincent, "there was no fire in my eye when I first looked on you." But there was glee in her eye as she teased him.

"Hush, *habibti*, there is fire in the tale, and thus it was so. A lie is only a story that nobody yet knows. Besides, you are a laundress, not the Caliph's sister."

And Ayesha fell silent and looked down.

Zami began his tale, watching the princess ever and again. He recounted the legend of the love between Khosrow, Prince of Persia, and Shirin, Princess of Armenia. The audience, of course, knew the tale well, and nodded sagely as Zami described how Khosrow's dead grandfather appeared to him in a vision. The spirit prophesied that he would meet and marry a maiden named Shirin.

Eager for the heart of the tale, the courtiers leant forward, urging on the emissary that Khosrow sent to Armenia to find Shirin. "You have forgotten the portrait," *someone called to the storyteller,*

"Never," *Zami said with a smile, and recounted how Shirin fell in love with Khosrow's portrait carried by the emissary.*

The listeners yielded a sigh as the emissary returned and reported Shirin's flawless beauty. They settled into the rhythm of the story as Khosrow set off to find and wed the maiden. They knew what was coming, but still they chuckled when Zami got to the comedy of errors where the lovers first see each other. Shirin bathing naked in a stream, washing her flowing hair. Khosrow smitten, thinking her the most beautiful woman he had ever laid eyes on.

But, as the audience expected, he didn't know this was the Princess of Armenia and, though she saw the Prince, she had no idea it was him because he was dressed in peasant clothes.

The ill-fated lovers crossed paths only briefly, travelling in opposite directions. When Khosrow arrived, dusty and expectant at the palace, he was told that Shirin has departed, in search of her Prince. The rueful chuckles of his listeners faded as Zami told of the messenger arriving with news that Khosrow's father had died. As was his duty, the Prince hurried home to assume the crown.

But his travails were far from done. Khosrow was overthrown by a scheming general, and forced to seek refuge in

Armenia. There, he at last found Shirin, and the love between the pair was true. Shirin, however, could not marry him until he regained his throne.

Zami's tone grew laboured and slow as Khosrow set off to win back his country. In Constantinople the Prince gained the support of the Caesar for his campaign. But the price of the alliance was high – he was forced to marry the Caesar's daughter, Mariam. Oh cruel fate, and fickle offspring as Mariam bore him a son! Breath hissed from the pursed lips of the audience.

The trials and tribulations, the twists and turns of the military campaign were agonising. At last Zami's hero defeated the usurper and sat again on the Peacock Throne. In the many years of suffering, Khosrow's son had grown to manhood and Mariam had died. Shirin rushed to his side. Nothing now stood in the way of the lovers. Nothing that is, but the jealous son who wanted Shirin for himself. Zami's voice rose, sharp as a blade, to the ribbed roof of the hall. Each word hammered home as the treacherous blade struck and struck again until brave Khosrow lay dead at his child's feet. At each stab, the listeners bled a gasp. Rather than yield to the monstrous assassin, Shirin seized the blade and plunged it into her own heart.

The shadows lengthened and night fell as Zami recounted the ancient tale. Zami looked, and silent tears were coursing down Ayesha's cheek.

Don Vincent looked, and silent tears were coursing down his wife's cheek.

The Caliph too was dewy-eyed, and a courtier passed him a kerchief. His Magnificence blew his nose with a great trumpeting.

"Well, upon my soul," the ruler said, "I have never heard the tale of Shirin and Khosrow told so well. There is no sweeter *story. And Shirin is a model to all women, choosing death rather than dishonour."*

Zami became a favourite at court, and little by little ascended to the status of counsellor to the Caliph. He learned all the state's secrets and military dispositions. This knowledge would be priceless to Zami's master.

But all in good time, for His Magnificence spoke as they walked together in the pleasure garden, saying, "You are the most steadfast of my confidantes, the most loyal of my subjects. What would you ask of me? If it is in my power, I will grant it."

Zami thought about the locked tower and the treasures it contained. And they were as nothing, less than the dust upon the ground.

"Your sister, Sire. I would wed her, for she is beautiful as Shirin and as pure."

With Ayesha by his side, what could Zami not accomplish? But there was no hurry, time there was aplenty.

And the Caliph embraced him with tears in his eyes, and called him son.

Ayesha brought the roasted capon to Don Vincent, who carved for them succulent slices, dripping with juice.

"Oh how lovely, how perfect," she said. "And did they marry?"

"They did," Don Vincent agreed.

"And did they live happily ever after?"

"They did."

"And did Zami go back to his master with the Caliph's secrets?"

Don Vincent thought about that for long moments as he bit and chewed the meat. Juice ran down his chin, and Ayesha wiped it with a cloth and they kissed.

"Well?" she asked.

"I do not know for sure," Don Vincent said. "I think perhaps he did not."

CHAPTER 14

The café in Brookhurst became a place of magic, a realm out of space and time where all the rules were different.

Zami knew that a story is an illusion you control. It imposes order on chaos. The danger is getting lost in the tale.

"Don't you have a job you need to be at?" Ayesha asked in the third week they shared coffee and cake.

"Wednesday is my afternoon off, like you."

"What is it you do? I know nothing about you."

"You see everything important. That we share a delight in the stars, in verse, and in each other's company."

Ayesha stirred her coffee, the spoon going round and round, making waves of brown foam against the side of the white cup.

She lifted an eyebrow. "That's not really an answer is it? Maybe it's a secret? I get it, you could tell me but you'd have to kill me afterwards."

Each man kills the thing he loves, Zami thought.

"I could never hurt you, Ayesha."

"My brothers would kill me, if they found us together." Her tone was flat, as if she was conveying an obvious fact.

"That seems a bit extreme. Wouldn't we have to make love or something first?"

"When we do, they will."

Not if, when. The world paused. A sudden silence fell, an intimate silence, but full of the echoes of words unspoken.

Ayesha blushed. "I'm sorry, I don't know what made me say that."

She gazed at him, imploring, her hand flat on the table between them. A rift tore in reality, he on one side, she on the other. He reached out. Her eyes followed the movement and then flicked back to his face. The nod might just have been a bashful lowering of her gaze, or perhaps it was assent. Zami's hand dropped to cover hers.

Crow averts his good eye, and the pair are invisible.

Ayesha's flesh was cool, the bones fine as a bird's leg under his fingers. Zami felt his hand grow warm. He hadn't known a palm could blush and hoped it wasn't sweating. Almost, he withdrew his touch, so the moist embrace wouldn't repulse her. But she lifted her gaze to his, and her grateful smile gave him resolve.

The words spoken now would start a new story – either way the choice was unavoidable. "We both understand what made you say that, Ayesha. You had the courage to speak what's there between us. Yes, we will make love. Yes, and yes. I want that."

A flood of expressions flashed across the face Ayesha bent to him. Joy he recognised, and fear, and doubt and a narrowing of the eyes that might have been calculation, and many more he didn't recognise or possess names for. The rift closed and her hand was still under his.

"And I won't let Rashid and Afaq hurt you," Zami said. "They'll never find out."

"People talk. Even here, someone who recognises me might see us."

"Then we'll go somewhere else, to a land far, far away where nobody knows us."

"Do you think I'm brazen, Zami? I am, aren't I?"

The shake of his head was emphatic. "No, I think you're wonderful. Brave and truthful."

And still their hands were clasped. Ayesha was the first to notice. She slid her hand away, eyes darting round the surrounding tables and then to the street beyond the window.

Nobody was watching. They were invisible.

"Zami, nobody has ever treated me like you do. You take me seriously, speak to me as an equal. Do you know how special that is? No, of course you don't. How could you? You're a man, and you're white."

There was more sadness than bitterness in her words, but still they stung.

"I can try," he said. "Please explain."

"We hover between two worlds. I mean us British Pakistani women. And we fit in neither world. Not the villages of our parents, nor the liberties of our white sisters. Our fathers bring us up to be dutiful, obedient, docile. But society tells us we are free. How can we be both free and docile? The contradiction tears us apart."

"Then be free, why can't you?"

"Freedom isn't so easy, Zami. To be free, you have to have strong roots. Are the white women free? I see them in the streets on a Friday night, falling-down drunk, vulgar, out of control. If that's freedom, it's nothing I want. Maybe we're not so different after all. Maybe, like me, they don't really know where they fit either."

Not knowing where you fitted. Yes, that he understood. He nodded and smiled with his eyes.

"The Muslim community doesn't give women the same chances as men. My brothers get to study, but I have to mind the shop. Still, it's my community, my roots. Do you understand?"

"No, not really. That's not Islam."

Her laugh was bitter. "No, it's not Islam, it's men. The Qu'ran promises women equality in life, education, property, free choice. But men's law says the woman's life is in the home. The Salafists say a woman in the male domain is a moral danger. But the Prophet, peace be upon him, used to teach women along with men. You say I'm brave, but I'm not. I don't have the courage to chop my own roots off. I have two faces – the one I show the world, and the one for me. They are not the same."

"Do you really believe your brothers would do you in?"

"Yes. Honour is everything to us."

The way she said "us" encompassed the world, her world – a cruel realm that sucked out joy and left only the shrivelled husk of duty.

And then Zami understood the source of the sadness that lived within her. She had a keen intellect and a ravenous curiosity. In another universe, she wouldn't have been just a shop girl. But that life was forever beyond her grasp. Yes, she could leave and begin a new life, be someone else. But that someone would still be a shop girl. No university would ever hone the edge of that eager curiosity or slake that thirst. She would never stride a stage and wow an audience.

"How would they kill you?" It was an attempt at dark humour, macabre levity, but it failed.

The sadness deepened in Ayesha's eyes. "Perhaps they'd stone me. Or maybe they'd strap a suicide belt to me and blow me up. It would take a dramatic gesture to erase the shame. Love is the enemy of honour."

A suicide belt! Where did Rashid and Afaq learn to make a suicide belt? How much did she fathom about her brothers' weekend jaunts?

Her anguish hurt him, so much that he wanted to take her in his arms and soothe the wound. Better words, he needed better words. A story came to him.

"Ayesha's brothers encouraged the liaison. For Don Vincent was a devout Muslim."

"What? What are you talking about?"

"You haven't heard the story of Don Vincent and Ayesha? Then let me tell you, *habibti*. It takes place many, many years ago in Moorish Spain."

"Al Andalus," she corrected.

"Well, Don Vincent was a student from Salamanca, a well-born lad, clever, charming and handsome. In the summers he went wandering the roads of Iberia, travelling from town to town with his lute, singing to the crowds, and reciting stories. Throughout the land, his voice had no equal, neither in Catholic Spain, nor among the Moors. And then he arrived in Granada."

Gradually the tightness around Ayesha's eyes loosened and the frown lines settled. She was spell-bound by the legend. Joy radiated from her face, tangible as a saint's halo, and the surrounding world faded into shadow.

He recounted the adventure of the guarded tower, the ghost soldier, the gluttonous priest and the chaste girl.

He told of the vanishing treasure and the real treasure Don Vincent found in Ayesha. When he finished, Ayesha sighed.

"So that's what you do for a living," she joked. "You're a storyteller."

"I am."

"And they give storytellers Wednesday afternoon off?"

"Only to recite for private audiences."

They were careful. They caught separate trains back home. Zami remained in the café while Ayesha caught the first train. Even after she had gone, the radiance lingered at their table.

"Hello, Vince me old mate." Tommy slid into the seat opposite, placing a cup of tea and a choux bun in front of him.

The world holds a great stillness, like the quiet of winter. It is terribly cold. Ishtar cries "Danger!" Crow sneers, "They know you're here". Zami laces his fingers.

Tommy laughed. It wasn't a kind laugh. "Close your mouth. You look like the village idiot."

"What?"

"I waited until your friend had gone." There was a knowing sneer at the word *friend*. "Didn't want to embarrass you, did I? She's quite a looker, if you like dark meat."

Zami understood Tommy was enjoying himself. Tommy always liked it when he had something on his colleagues.

"What?"

"For fuck's sake, stop saying 'what,' Vince. You didn't report in. There were no messages in the drop, so I came looking for you. Had to, you made me."

Crow laughs.

"Okay."

Tommy leant back in his chair, hands laced behind his head. "So, how's the investigation going, Vince? People are getting worried. Time is running out."

Malachi whispers, insidious as a knife, "How little separates us from what we fear."

"It's going fine, don't you worry, Tommy. I've got it all under control."

"Don't seem that way to me. You haven't made a drop in days. We were concerned you might have met with some mischief."

Crow caws, "What did he mean by mischief?"

"She's not a friend – she's a source."

"Source of what though, eh? Are you getting any there?"

"Intelligence, you fuckwit. Information."

"Okay, give. What did she tell you?"

What had she told him? Think.

"Rashid and Afaq are attending weapons training camps at the weekends. How to make and use suicide belts."

"She told you that?"

"Yes."

"Welly, welly, well. This is news. Nothing like that is showing up on Rashid's internet activity."

"You're monitoring his traffic?"

"Yup, we infected his computer with spyware. The moron opened the e-mail and now we can see it all."

"Are you crazy? If he finds it, he'll guess he's under surveillance."

Tommy lunged, hands on the edge of the table bracing himself as he thrust his face into Zami's. "Well, you should have reported in, shouldn't you?"

Malachi spreads his wings, sinews turning great gears. "You think of fear and you imagine a sudden shape in the underbrush, a howl in the night. If only it were that simple."

"Get over it, Tommy. I'm reporting now. If you hadn't been stupid enough to follow me, where we can be seen together, I'd have dropped you a note tonight."

"Do you have a target? What they're planning to hit?"

"Not yet. I'm working on it."

Tommy tapped a fork against his teeth, gaze unblinkingly fixed on Zami.

"He doesn't believe you," Malachi taunts. "We can smell your stink, your fear."

What the fuck was Malachi doing here? Was he imagining this?

"You wouldn't be going bush on me, would you, me old mate?"

How like Tommy that was – a phrase he'd liked and adopted from the old colonials when they were both nippers. Who even understood these days what "going bush" meant?

The derision drips from Malachi's mouth like venom. "Contemptuous people should take care not to be contemptible themselves. You're pathetic, rotten."

"Don't you sometimes just want the noise to stop?" Ishtar is sympathetic. And, yes, he does want it to stop.

"No, Tommy, I'm not going bush," Zami made mocking hooks in the air with his fingers around the phrase.

"Glad to hear it, mate. You did look proper cosy with that bint."

Zami's fists balled by his waist and his heart raced.

How did Tommy always do this to him? Always find his weak spots? He had to win; he had to.

CHAPTER 15

"Islam," Rashid said, "announces the freedom of man from servitude to other men. This is what Qutb teaches us. What does that mean, brothers?"

Zami looked at the cover of his study text, seeking an answer. Fouad scratched his chin. A bus rumbled by in the world outside. The little room in the community centre was warm and stuffy, like the parlour of an aging relative.

"It means only Islam can make us free," Abdul Bari said.

"Yes," said Rashid, "but it means more. If you follow the logic, therefore, the Islamic state opposes all other forms of government. These can only express the dominion of man over man, and the servitude of one human being to another."

When Rashid became swept up, in an idea or a verse, the street argot dropped away.

"I didn't see that in the chapter we read," Zami said.

"Right, brother Zami, it isn't. Qutb was on a journey, wasn't he? Just after the Second World War he went to America and was shocked by the degeneracy he saw there. He found the women to be shameless and the men brutes."

Rashid picked up another book and flourished it like a standard. "This is what he wrote afterwards. *The America I Have Seen*. It could be England today."

His tongue slowly lapped his lips in a gesture Zami found peculiarly sensuous. Then he quoted:

"*The American girl is well acquainted with her body's seductive capacity. She knows it lies in the face, and in expressive eyes, and thirsty lips. She knows seductiveness lies in the round breasts, the full buttocks, and in the shapely thighs, sleek legs – and she shows all this and does not hide it.*"

Afaq shifted uneasy in his seat and Abdul Bari mirrored his squirm. The others looked down at the floor with sly grins. Zami wanted to laugh. It sounded so much like an old-fashioned fire and brimstone sermon. He wondered what Qutb's sex life had been like.

"The eternal Eve," Zami said.

"Not in Islam, brother," Afaq said. "That's the Christian Eve. Adam and Hawwa bore equal blame for eating the forbidden fruit. But Allah forgave them. The Christians believe God cast them out of the Garden as a punishment, but the Qu'ran teaches us that He always intended the Earth as our home."

Rashid continued. "When he left America, Qutb began to explore what freedom really meant. Just after Nasser overthrew the corrupt king in Egypt, he wrote the book we're reading, *Social Justice in Islam*. The conclusion about true freedom comes from his last book the one he wrote before the Nasserites executed him."

Zami remembered what he was there for. "So, if Islam is incompatible with all other forms of government, what must Muslims do?"

Rashid gazed at the ceiling, then smiled and fixed Zami with an unblinking stare. It was like being studied by a hawk. "What do you think, brother? What do you say Muslims must do?"

How provocative to be? Zami was trapped in a moment of indecision that belonged wholly to Vince.

A voice in his head mocked. *Shut up, Vince. You're weak.*

"Work for an Islamic state," Zami said.

"Fight for an Islamic state," Abdul Bari corrected.

"Does working have to mean fighting?" Zami asked.

"The *kufar* will never just abandon power," Abdul Bari said.

Now. Now, we come to it. Yes.

Rashid flicked his hand in dismissal. "Whether Muslims have to fight *jihad*, or whether they can change the world through preaching is a matter of tactics. It all depends on the circumstances we face. The main thing is what does it mean to be an Islamic state?"

That was disappointing.

"I like what Qutb says about social justice," Afaq said.

Rashid nodded. "That's the point. Muslims have to oppose any system that enslaves men to other men. We serve only Allah. A truly Islamic society will have no rulers, Muslims don't need no judges or police to obey divine law."

Fouad wrinkled his brow. "How's that going to work? There'll always be people who thieve."

"Families don't need police to deal with bad people. We're all one family and we'll sort out bad people by ourselves." That was the normally reticent Iqbal.

Rashid nodded in approval. "Right, brother."

But Fouad wasn't convinced. "Sounds sort of anarchist to me."

Iqbal's reply was swift. "The anarchists don't believe in Allah, do they? Not in any kind of God."

Fouad busied himself with some ear wax, but Zami could see from the frown he didn't feel this answered his point.

"But it is kind of revolutionary," Zami said, filling the silence.

Why do you always think silences are your fault?

Rashid shrugged. "If you want to see it that way."

"So," Zami persisted, "doesn't that mean we need a revolution to build the perfect society? Like the Caliphate did?"

The temperature in the room seemed to plummet. Everyone round the table leaned forward at attention.

"We don't have nothing to do with ISIS," Rashid said.

Six pairs of eyes scrutinised Zami.

"No, no. Of course. I just meant a revolution like they did. What Abdul Bari said."

Rashid wasn't to be placated. Suspicion darkened his eyes. "Why you talking about Islamic State?"

Zami stumbles in the fog. He can't tell where he is. Familiar landscapes are strange. A figure stands sentinel by the tower, silhouetted against the mist.

Get away from me!

"I didn't mean nothing."

"You ask a lot of questions about *jihad*. What's going on, brother?"

"Nothing, nothing. Honest."

Abdul Bari pitched in, turning to Rashid. "What do we really know about Zami?"

Rashid put both hands on the table and leaned forward. "Yes, what do we really know about you, brother Zami?"

Every victory brought him closer to defeat. The room darkened and narrowed to a corridor. He felt hands sprouting from the walls, clawing at him.

"You think he's like an agent or something?" Fouad asked.

Abdul Bari was unsure. "But it was him got us out of the cop shop, wasn't it?"

A light at the end of the tunnel? Or just an oncoming train?

"Who are you, Zami?" Rashid asked.

"What you see is what you get," Zami said. "There are no secrets."

He turned to Fouad. "I'm not an agent."

Rashid stroked his beard, combing his fingers through it. "Well you ask a lot of questions."

"How else will I learn? Allah loves the ignorant, for He loves it when we strive for knowledge."

Afaq laughed. "Now that sounds like something my sister would say."

Rashid's unblinking stare transfixed Zami

"I don't trust him," said Fouad.

"Well I do." *At least Afaq defended him! Blessed Afaq.*

In the labyrinth, some turns ended blind, while other paths circled forever. And at the centre slept a beast. Zami could not tell where the entrance was anymore. The ball of yarn he had unrolled to find his way out crossed and recrossed other traces. The walls themselves seemed to move around, for several threads ran into and through barricades.

Wheeling round a blind corner, Abdul Bari went to battle for him, maybe because he felt a debt or maybe too because he saw nothing wrong with radical beliefs. But, advancing down another corridor, Fouad, his brother, was more suspicious. Here, distrust made sense – you never knew whether a creature's shape reflected its true nature.

Afaq held the middle, demanding fairness. The other members of the group startled and skittered, like small prey. From on high, Rashid stroked his beard and watched as the combat raged.

Fouad said, "He would say that, wouldn't he, if he was a plant?"

Abdul Bari spread his hands. "He would say that too, if he was innocent."

Afaq asked, "Why would a plant have saved us?"

Fouad was not to be convinced. "That's exactly what an agent would do."

Innocence and guilt. The watcher observed, impassive, unmoving. It seemed to Zami that even his eyes didn't blink as he collated all the versions into an official narrative.

At last, Rashid stirred. "Maybe, brother Zami, it would be better if you left the group." He spoke slowly and, it seemed, with sadness. "I can't tell what's right here. But we have to be able to trust each other, that's what I know."

"Can we vote on it?" Zami asked.

Dark wings enfold him, He smells Malachi's stench, like rotting meat in the jaws of a jackal. "You're no use, boy. You can't win. You always lose."

No. You're not here, Malachi. You're not real. Go away!

Rashid's eyes turned cold. "This ain't a *kufar* democracy, brother. It's Allah's way, not man's way, innit?"

Zami pushed back his chair and stood. It seemed to take a long time. Nobody spoke as he slunk to the door. He turned the handle, then paused and looked back at Rashid.

"I am not a liar."

CHAPTER 16

Zami told many tales to those who would listen. As the world closed in, his stories grew darker. One was of the Queen of Heaven who birthed and abandoned him.

Ishtar looks out over the dun walls of Uruk, stabbing sword clenched in her fist, as she watches the battle on the sands below. The silver-on-black eight-pointed banner flutters over the towers. Her Bull of Heaven stamps great hooves, and the earth itself trembles. A tower splinters and crumbles at the concussion.

Undaunted, Malachi's captain vaults over the Bull's horns, somersaulting on the beast's back and landing, sure-footed behind it. *How lithe the boy is*, Ishtar thinks despite herself, *how beautiful.*

Malachi spreads vast wings, darkening the sky. He beats his chest.

"Ishtar," he thunders, "give back what is mine."

Once, Uruk had been Malachi's city, until she seized it.

That was her way. In the beginning of time, when Enki, Lord of the Earth, wrote the cosmic order, she had no domain and few powers. What she now possessed, she had taken. Her first theft was from the tree of love, which grows in Kur, the underworld. Young and innocent she entered its dark realm. There she ate of the tree's fruit and became the Goddess of Sex, expert in the ways of love. Her priests sing, "The pearls of a prostitute are placed around your neck, and you are likely to snatch a man from the tavern."

Then she held a drinking bout with Enki, stealing the powers of civilisation, both good and ill: Truth, Victory, and Counsel, Writing and Weaving, Law, Priestly Offices, Kingship, and Prostitution.

Like the leech, she absorbed all the abilities of her mother, Anatu, leaving her an empty husk, and usurped the domain of her father Anu, god of the Sky. Now Ishtar possesses dominion over Love and Fertility, War, Justice, and Rule. Thus did she become Queen of Heaven.

"Give me my city," Malachi demands again.

Ishtar leans over the battlements and makes a vulgar gesture. "Never, husband. Take it, if you are man enough."

"Nobody is man enough for you, wife," Malachi retorts. "You consume and betray all your lovers. Listen while I tell the tale of your mates. There was Tammuz, the lover of your youth, for him you decreed wailing, year after year. You loved the many-coloured lilac-breasted roller, but still you struck and broke his wing. You have loved the stallion magnificent in battle, and for him you decreed the whip and spur and a thong. You have loved the shepherd of the flock; he made meal-cake for you day after day and killed kids for your sake. You struck and turned him into a wolf; now his own herd-boys chase him away and his own hounds worry his flanks. You are a cruel and capricious lover, Ishtar."

Then Malachi's captain wrestles the Bull of Heaven, while the besieging army cheers. For a day and a night the pair fight. The Beast yields a bellow of anguish that shivers the sky, as the youth tears off its hind flank. He waves the thigh like a banner and shouts at Ishtar, "If I could lay my hands on you, it is this I should do to you, and lash your entrails to your side."

With a scream of rage, Ishtar unleashes fire and fury. The Warrior Queen of Heaven strikes the captain dead. Plagues ravage Malachi's army. Water turns to blood. The battle is terrible but, in the end, her husband prevails: she abandons the city and her son, Zami.

While Malachi gloats, Ishtar flees to Kur. This is the domain of her sister, Ereshkigal, whose consort the Bull of Heaven was. Ishtar goes to console her. Perhaps, she also goes to add a new realm to her conquests and to prepare her revenge on Malachi.

The cavernous underworld is a drear and shadowy version of the world of the living. Apart from official messengers, nobody, god or mortal, may enter Kur and leave again. None save Ishtar, for she is Venus, the evening star and the morning star, setting in the west only to rise again in the east. Yet, even for her, the journey is perilous, and she instructs her vassals to plead with the gods for her release if she does not return in three days. She dresses in her finery. Each item carries one of the powers she stole from Enki – a ladyship robe and a turban over a ceremonial wig, a carnelian necklace and pectoral, beads upon her breast and a gold ring on her finger. She bears a lapis lazuli measuring rod, with which to apportion the thread of life to each.

The great entry gate of Kur is heavy and forbidding, carved with the heads of kings and farmers, and embossed with ancient runes in a tongue none now speak. The way is held by Neti, the gatekeeper of the underworld.

"What is your business here?" he asks.

Ishtar is angered and is haughty in her demand to him. "I am Ishtar, the Queen of Heaven. I have come to share the funeral rites of my sister's husband. If you do not open the gate for me to come in, I shall smash the door and shatter the bolt. I am Innana. I shall crush the doorpost and overturn the door. I am Astarte. I shall raise up the dead and they shall eat the living. I have many names, and the dead shall outnumber the living."

The gatekeeper hurries to Ereshkigal to inform her that her sister is at the gate. The Queen of the Underworld orders him to let Ishtar in, but that she should be treated according to the ancient rites. He returns to the door and bids Ishtar to enter, but tells her she must leave her measuring rod.

She narrows her eyes. "Oh? Why?"

Neti shrugs. "This is just the way of the realm."

Ishtar has no choice but to comply, and Neti opens the gate. The way is dark, and small bones crunch underfoot. In the gloom, winged creatures caw and sweep down at her. Again a gate bars further passage, and again Neti tells her she must abandon an article, this time her gold ring. She passes seven gates, and at each she yields an item of clothing or adornment, disrobing of one power after another. She arrives, naked and proud, at her sister's throne.

"Why sister, what a surprise," says Ereshkigal. "To what do I owe the pleasure?"

Ishtar settles on the throne of the underworld and says, "I am here to grieve with you for the death of your husband, the Bull of Heaven, who was slain by Malachi's captain."

Ereshkigal frowns, both at her sister's temerity in sitting the throne of Kur, and at her words. "But my husband is Nergal, the god of plagues. You know this. I trust not your purpose here."

The Queen of the Underworld summons the seven judges of her realm to render decision against Ishtar for her pride and stealth. They look upon her, and it is the look of death. They speak to her in the tone of anger. In a great shout, they give judgement, and it is the shout of heavy guilt. Ishtar is without her powers and is turned into a corpse. The corpse is hung in the wind on a hook. All sex stops on earth.

Three days and three nights pass, and Ishtar's handmaiden, as instructed, appeals for help. Enki agrees and creates two messengers from the dirt under the gods' fingernails. They descend to Kur and find Ereshkigal suffering the agony of fever, her body twisted like a woman in childbirth. In return for healing her, they request Ishtar's corpse. Sprinkled with the bread and water of life, the ailing goddess revives.

Ishtar passes back through the seven gates, receiving at each the article she had shed. She stands at the entrance gates, resplendent again in all her powers. But her sister sends demons after her.

The captain of the demons is tall and fierce and spreads leathery wings to block her way. She is reminded of Malachi, and she wonders at the small sadness that accompanies the memory. After all, having a husband is good.

"None can leave the underworld," says the captain, "unless another enters in their stead." He bares his teeth.

"Who would you have me give up?" asks Ishtar, looking at Enki's two messengers.

The demon laughs. It is not a pleasant laugh and sets the cavernous mouth of Kur tolling like a bell. "Not them," he says, "they are creatures of dirt. Ereshkigal demands a god to take your place. She demands your son, Zami."

The demons take wing, wheeling over the gate and then disappearing into the light. They return with Zami, struggling in a bag made from the paunch of the Bull of Heaven. The boy is cut loose, though a demons holds each arm.

Zami cries piteously. "Mother, don't do this. You cannot abandon your own son to the shadow of Kur."

The demons release their grip, and Zami falls at his mother's feet.

Ishtar, hands on hips, looks him up and down. "You are growing into a pretty young man."

"Then save me, as a mother should." Zami laces his fingers in entreaty.

The Queen of Heaven laughs, and the sound is more terrible than the demon's mirth. "You mistake to whom you are talking, lad. Enki did not grant me a mother's love. I am Aphrodite, goddess of love, not of maternity, nor of marriage. I have no such fine sensibilities."

She turns to the demon captain, nodding, and Zami is marched down into the murk.

Ages pass. Storms scud across the sky, weathering great mountains to toothless stubs. Oceans rise and cover the earth and recede again. At last, the land quivers. A finger pokes through, then a hand. Lungs suck air, and Zami crawls out onto the soil. The sun breaks through. Corn ripens. Shepherds tend their new lambs and peasant girls dance around maypoles. Then a great clawed fist bursts through the crust of the world, seizes Zami, and drags him back to the underworld. Leaves fall and ice covers the waters until it is Zami's time to escape again.

CHAPTER 17

The sun draped an arm over Zami's shoulders. Ayesha walked proud by his side through the leafy avenues of Brookhurst cemetery. Ishtar asks the Green Man to cast a protective spell around them.

He handed Ayesha the package and watched, eager with anticipation, as she tore off the crepe paper wrapping. "Well, what do you think?"

The colour was mauve, not one he'd ever seen her wear, but he'd thought it regal. The swirling butterfly pattern had called to him when he saw the hijab on the market stall. It had brought with it a sudden sharp recall of his mother's Paisley shawl. When he held it, running it through his fingers, it had tickled like Ayesha's hair.

"It's," she held it up, turning it to the light, "lovely." It looked garish as she held it against the azure of her shalwar kameez. "Thank you, Zami."

"You hate it, don't you?" he asked, sorrowed.

"No, no. Really. You've never bought me a gift before. Thank you, I'll treasure it."

Her smile was strained, and she made no move to remove her hijab and try his gift on. He was charmed by the grace of her social lie.

Zami reached out, and she was fully in the hand that took his.

She had been dismayed at first when he told her about being banished from the study group, but not surprised.

"Yes, they're so paranoid about security," she said.

"Given what they're up to, that makes sense."

"What? What are they up to?"

"Weapons training, you know?" he said.

She stiffened, and her eyes went wide. "I was afraid of that. Oh God, what to do? Rashid is all sharp edges. He doesn't understand how to compromise. Even as a boy he was like that, so sure he was right and everyone else was wrong."

"And Afaq follows?"

"Yes, he idolises his older brother. Rashid was always the leader."

"I admire him too." Zami slumped.

"To the point of joining them for weapons training, and learning how to kill? You're not a killer, Zami."

But there are many ways to kill, and each man kills the thing he loves.

Zami shrugged. "I can understand Rashid's anger. We talked about it."

"But would you kill?"

"If I believed it was my duty, yes."

"Then I have to convince you it's your duty not to kill innocents. If you kill an innocent, it's as bad as if you'd killed the whole of humanity. The Qu'ran is very clear about this."

Zami wasn't sure that any holy book was clear about anything. Ambiguity seemed to lie at the core of any successful religion. But he didn't contradict her.

"Zami, what should I do? Is it my duty to report them? But how can I turn my own brothers in? I don't know what's right here."

He was quick to ease her conscience, taking her hand again. "You can't, *habibti*, you mustn't. There's no saying they've done anything or are planning anything. My guess? It's all talk."

"Do you really think so? Yes, yes maybe. But, I don't know. If they did do something, something terrible, how could I live with myself? You can't know for certain what they're up to. Can you?"

He exhaled. A long breath. "Maybe there's a way we can find out. If I could get back into the study group, I could check. And tell you. Then you could decide what's best. If you dob them in now, they'll suffer. Their friends too. And you and me, maybe."

Her hand fluttered in his, a trapped bird, and she looked up, searching his eyes. "That's true. We don't know. People like us shouldn't lightly invite the state to notice them. Yes, I'm sure you're right."

He squeezed her hand, perhaps a little harder than he'd intended.

"Did you really want to go back into Rashid's study group?" she asked.

"Yes, very much. I was learning a lot."

She looked as if she doubted there was anything to learn in the group, but her tone remained sympathetic. "I could talk to him. He pretends women are beneath him, but really he respects me."

"That would be great, Ayesha. But what if it gets you into trouble? What if it makes him suspect us?"

"I'm not stupid, Zami. I know how to handle him. What you do with Rashid is plant seeds, and when they grow, he believes the whole idea was his."

"What seed will you plant?"

Planting seeds. Yes, Zami understood that. Small nudges made people do what you wanted whereas shoving them only made them stubborn.

"I can't tell yet. What happened? Why did he throw you out of the study group? Which flower do I need?"

"More a hulking great marrow than a dainty flower, I'd say."

The joke wasn't a great one, but she laughed at his play with the metaphor and he laughed with her.

Zami continued. "I said something about ISIS and they all got jittery. It was completely innocent, but they decided I was a spy, might be a spy."

"You? A spy? Sleeping with the suspect's sister – that wouldn't be hugely discreet."

"I'm not sleeping with you."

"No, but you will."

Zami halted in his tracks. A bird stopped in mid-call. A dandelion puffball hovered motionless, the sun shining white fire through its hairs.

He had been startled, at first, by her boldness. Later, he came to learn Ayesha was like that, trying on identities like hats. She just came out with things: bold and dangerous and lovely things.

He smiled. She smiled and didn't lower her eyes. When he reached for her, then she did look down and buried her face against his shoulder. He held her. After a time, he lifted her chin with a finger. The kiss was inevitable, sweet and lingering. The moment extended out into the far future. Her heart beat against his.

And then he sensed it. The bird, the one-eyed crow that had protected him from Tommy in the graveyard, was there, fluttering inside her. He felt it against his chest. Nothing else moved but that talisman in her breast, and their lips, and his hands on her back. The good, loamy scent of her filled his nostrils, the spicy taste of her mouth tingled on his tongue.

Confessing their lust to Rashid didn't seem the surest way of getting her brother to trust him, but Zami kept silent. This wasn't the moment for sarcasm.

She seemed to sense his idea and, breaking the kiss, held his face between her hands. "Silly! Of course I'm not going to tell Rashid about us."

"So what will you say?"

She shrugged and laughed. "I'll think of something"

They walked, and they talked about everything and nothing, just for the pleasure of hearing each other and sharing. The far end of the graveyard was overgrown, full of secret passages and hidden burrows. And nothing that grew there or slept there was mean or threatening. Insects buzzed and hummed, birds called, the very earth flexed and breathed.

"Something's happening," Ishtar says.

Go away, Ishtar. You're not real. Leave me in peace.

Ayesha was looking at him strangely. "Are you alright?" she asked. "You went away."

"Never better," Zami said, and he put his arms around her.

Lying safe together in a grotto, his arms went around her, and the branches around them. They exchanged stories and speculations, each more fanciful than the last.

"What if …"

Zami loved any conversation that started that way. It conjured up the most delightful fairy tales and the deepest philosophy.

"What if the whole universe is a story?" she said.

"Okay," he said, "so who's telling it?"

"Nobody. There's no narrator and no listeners, only the story."

That's why he'd come to adore her. She lived in a different world from other people: more surprising, more complicated.

"So how does that work?" he asked.

"The story tells itself. Oh, like frames in a movie. When you've seen the previous frame, you can guess at what comes next."

"Perhaps we can change the plot then? If we guess differently?"

A different narrative! In which Rashid and Afaq were benign, and in which Tommy was permanently loaned to the Falklands police. A life in which the voices in his head fell silent.

He feels Ishtar's fury, as she wheels away. For Ishtar, goddess of love and war, was a jealous god. Yet he does not mourn her loss, for he has Khawla Bint al-Azwar, Islamic warrior princess, by his side. With Khawla he could make new stories.

"We can only change the plot," she said, "if we exist, outside of it."

"Maybe there are many stories, as many as there are readers, each creating their own version of reality. How about that?"

Her brow creased in thought, and her lips pursed like a kiss, and his lips remembered the softness of them. "There are so many horrible things in the world. Why would we chose to imagine them? No, the story must be real, but we may not be."

After a moment, she added. "Or it could be that the story isn't real either. Perhaps nothing is, or everything is. Some scientists say we live in a universe in which all possibilities exist. Once I open the box, I see whether the cat is dead or alive. But you don't know until I tell you."

"The cat?"

"Schrödinger's cat – haven't you heard of it? The physicist Erwin Schrödinger imagined a cat in a box with a radioactive atom. If the atom decays and emits radiation, this triggers a switch and releases a poison that kills the cat. If the atom doesn't decay, the cat lives. Physics says both are equally likely and, until you open the box, the cat is both dead and alive."

"Ha! So the observer exists and creates the movie."

"Damn!" Her laugh was rueful.

The cat was both dead and alive. Rashid and Afaq were both guilty and innocent. Until he opened the box, all versions were true.

"Don't you like my version of the universe better than yours?" he asked. "In mine we can create our own story. What plot would you like?"

"Oh Zami, I'd like for us not to have to sneak around. Just to be happy together, like Don Vincent and his Ayesha."

The escape to Granada was born at that moment.

CHAPTER 18

In the great hall of the mosque, Rashid turned away as if he didn't see Zami. Most of the other study group members followed his lead. Afaq and Abdul Bari gave him uncomfortable glances and then looked down at the floor. Once, Afaq offered the slightest shrug, a silent apology, and a signalled plea for forgiveness. Only once.

In a moment of silent prayer, Malachi's mocking voice echoes like gunshots. "Home is a foreign land, and your loved ones are strangers. To understand your exile, you have to admit you were never really at home." Of Ishtar there is no sign.

But Ayesha's love he still had, a small parcel of dry land in the torrent. After Granada, they no longer met in Brookhurst but in his tiny flat on the west of town. Give him a place to stand and he would move the earth. No ghosts of his past, not Malachi nor Ishtar, would assail him with her to shield him.

Folk spilled out of the mosque, chatting and laughing. Zami was alone.

Walking helped him think. Over and over, like a shiny *dinar*, he turned the problem. If he didn't get back into the group, Tommy would pull him out of the operation. He reached the street market near the station and watched, without focusing, the vendors and the customers swirl in their dance. Vegetables, potted shrubs, and shirts changed hands, each transaction meaningful only on the smallest scale. He might try to exploit Ayesha's faith in him. She had offered. But this would only make Rashid oppose him more. She gave him strength, but was not the lever.

So, he had to prove his goodness by his own efforts. But how? Acts of charity and community service? An act of supreme daring to demonstrate his worth?

Zami contemplated placing a bomb to demonstrate his militancy: a small one, just a harmless little device. A bang, with no blood. Left somewhere empty, maybe a disused building, or a vacant carpark. He looked up the road to the curved concrete and glass sweep of the Peacock Shopping Centre. After closing, of course.

How did you make a bomb? Zami ran through the ingredients: explosives, detonator, timer, and container. A metal or plastic pipe would house it, and clocks were easily available. But where did you get explosives and a detonator?

Bleach, he thought he remembered mention of that – hydrogen peroxide. But you had to mix it with something else. What was it again? Some other household ingredient. That was the explosive in the 2005 London bombings and the 2015 Paris bombing if he recalled his terrorism briefings. TATP, yes that was it – tri-acetone tri-peroxide. Acetone. That was the other ingredient – nail polish remover. But what proportions? And how did you treat it?

He wished he'd paid more attention during the briefing. There was a catalyst involved, he thought. And he remembered terrorists called TATP the "mother of Satan" because of the risk of accidental detonation. Perhaps he'd better avoid TATP.

As a boy, he and a friend, Ron Kettlewell, had improvised explosives. Happy days! At fourteen, they'd blown up the school toilet block in the boys' playground. A hell of a bang, smoke pouring from both entrances, then the slow grind and crunch of falling masonry, kids running away, teachers running towards the debris. He recalled packing the explosive tightly to make it detonate rather than just flash. And that was where the risk of accidental detonation came in. So he must have known this stuff once.

In fact, it was Kettles who'd had the bomb-making knowledge. Zami had just been the lab assistant. What was it they'd used? Sugar and something else, something agricultural. Weed killer? Fertiliser? Yes, fertiliser. The IRA had used that too. But, since the "troubles", sales had been closely monitored. Surveillance probably covered acetone and peroxide too.

Not a good idea, then. In the first place, he didn't know exactly how to make a bomb, and in the second place, how would an ineffective explosion prove his zeal to Rashid? Do no harm, or complete the mission?

The laughter rolls like distant thunder, coming from everywhere at once, echoing off the station wall. "You're weak," says Malachi, "weak and useless."

Zami hunkers down, covering his ears. None of the shoppers looks up, or responds in any way to Malachi's taunts, or Zami's distress.

He slouched home, the jeer echoing in memory. The way seemed drab and long, full of shadows and overhanging buildings. Ayesha was there, still as a statue in the yard outside his ground-floor flat, surrounded by the debris of urban indifference, old crisp packets and beer cans. Even Ayesha couldn't lift his gloom, but he manufactured a welcoming smile.

"*Habibti,* I didn't know you were coming today. Sorry. Have you been waiting long? Maybe I should get you a key cut."

She pulled the silver-trimmed hijab tight about her head. "I wasn't coming today, *habibi*. But I was worried about you. I had to tell Papa I was going to visit a sick friend. And it seems I am."

She scanned his face, and he sensed she was detecting his mood. She seemed to be searching him for something. He unlocked the front door, passing ahead of her to set the water boiling for tea.

"Sorry," he said. "I've got the glums today."

She took his face between her hands. They were soft and warm. He hadn't been aware he was chilled.

"Oh, you're so cold," she said, massaging his cheeks. He remembered how his mother used to do that and felt like crying.

"What was it you were worrying about?"

"You, silly. You and Rashid."

The idea that someone was worried about him was precious, but it also peeled open his wound. "Oh? Why? There's nothing to worry about. I'm alright."

It was as if his attempted reassurance pressed a switch. She folded her arms. Her whole face drew tight as if his hands were purse strings. "Nothing? Don't take me for a fool. Weapons training isn't nothing. To kill innocents isn't nothing."

Zami took a step back and held up his hands. "Whoa, wait. I'm not going to kill anyone. Where did you get that idea?"

This only seemed to make her angrier. "It's not a joke, Zami. I got the idea from you. You told me my brothers are learning to kill. And you were in the group with them. I'm not stupid. I've been thinking about it all night. I suddenly realised what it all meant. It's a terrorist cell, isn't it? You're a terrorist. My brothers are terrorists. I was going to help you get back into the group, but I was wrong. I see that now."

He remained stilled, caught between a vortex inwards and a vortex outwards. Any word was perilous.

"Zami, you're new to Islam. You're young, attracted by derring-do as men are. But that's not Islam. Don't you see? It's not what the Prophet, peace be upon him, meant by *jihad*. I love you, but I can't be with someone who perverts our religion. I'm so sorry, but I just can't. We've already sinned enough."

Her eyes filled with tears. He moved to hold her. She reared back, shaking her head. Pebbles clogged his mouth, trapping the words. It was his duty to withhold the truth. That was why she hated him. His vision burned and his cheeks felt wet.

"How could you, Zami? You're gentle and sweet. When we made love, I saw the paradise gardens. And now you've ruined it, spat on our love. Everything in the garden is monstrous and dying. You stupid, stupid man."

She raised her hand and, for a moment, Zami thought she might hit him. But her brimming eyes held silent entreaty. She was waiting for him to say something, for some magic words that would make everything alright. If he said nothing, it was over. She might even decide to inform on him and her brothers. Somewhere there was a word that would stop everything shattering. He cast around for the spell. Would it suffice to deny he was a terrorist? Or would he have to tell her the truth? Rarely at a loss for words, he found none now, reached for her again and she again drew back.

"Open sesame," he said. But for that absurd phrase, no words came to mind. He laughed, and the sound was alien to him.

It was as if he'd slapped her. She spun on her heel and slammed the front door behind her.

CHAPTER 19

Zami stared at the impassive door, trying to figure out what had just happened. Then he raced into the street. Ayesha was already out of sight. His chest was tight, and he sucked in a deep breath, attempting to fill his lungs.

He ran to the junction with the main road, looking up and down the pavements. Hands on his thighs, he could only make the thin air come in short gasps. In the distance, he spotted a figure dressed in black, hurrying towards the town centre. He need to explain, to make it right.

"Ayesha," he tried to shout, but his voice lacked the power to carry.

The person turned the corner and was gone. Zami sprinted for the vanishing point, but had to stop, chest heaving, lungs burning. He leant, panting, on a lamppost.

The net curtain twitched in an adjacent dilapidated 1930s semi. A spectral face stared out. Zami waved his hand, perhaps in gratitude for concern, perhaps to make the watcher go away. The curtain fell back, and he was alone.

The world became slow and distant. He staggered past the county records library. Two men enjoyed cigarettes together on the portico. Inside, a tall woman carried a large book to a desk by the window. It seemed to be heavy, or perhaps fragile, because she handled it with some effort. A double-decker bus rumbled townward, children crammed at the top window seeming to point at him.

When he finally reached the corner, Ayesha had been swallowed by the crowd. Strangers thronged the market precinct. Zami pressed on, heading for Ayesha's corner shop. Somebody barged him, and he stumbled. His shoulder told him the collision hurt.

"Sorry," he said reflexively, even though it hadn't been his fault.

"Watch where you're going." The lad pushed his shaved head up close. He looked about eighteen. Zami smelled burger grease and chip fat.

"Oi! Look who it is," the skinhead called to his mates. "It's that white Mooslim. The one from when we done their mosque."

Four other lads crowded round. None was familiar, but the biggest one wore a hoodie with a red cross of Saint George on the chest. Zami had seen those at the attack on the mosque.

The youth pushed his face even closer. His words flecked Zami's cheek with spittle. "You're a disgrace, a fucking disgrace, mate. That's what you are. A traitor to the white race."

Zami looked left and right. The shoppers walked by, heads averted, leaving a space around them. One of the other lads tugged Zami's beard.

"Proper Mooslim, in't ee?"

Zami pushed through the knot of youths, and carried on across the plaza towards the station. He half turned and saw his tormentor standing, legs planted, staring at him. The boy brought two fingers to his eyes and, with a sneer, jabbed them at Zami, then repeated the threat.

Zami spun away, hurrying across the precinct. Finding Ayesha was all that mattered. His legs were leaden, and breath came in gasps as though he were running. Up ahead, he saw the swirl of a purple *abaya*. Had she been wearing purple?

He raced to catch up. But it wasn't her. He swiped a hand across his forehead, as if to erase his thoughts. A market vendor looked at him curiously.

He had lost Ayesha and he had lost Rashid and Afaq.

There had to be a way to get back into the study group. If he didn't, Tommy would end the operation and he'd lose everything. Though the bomb idea was wrong, there was something right in the notion if only he could fillet it out. What was it? If he wasn't skilled enough to detonate a device, might he offer up another sacrifice?

As he left the market square and passed the station entrance, Zami had to step into the road to avoid an emerging passenger. A car horn blared, and Zami jumped back onto the pavement. With a sense of unease, he remembered the day, months ago, when he had first seen Tommy coming out of the station with his rolling gait.

Tommy! He might offer up Tommy. Oh, that scheme flowed over his palate, delicious as wine! How he missed alcohol. Vince liked a drink, but to Zami booze was *haram*, forbidden. Give Tommy to Rashid and he'd have proved his loyalty and got rid of the sneering bastard at the same time. Zami's fists balled as he remembered Tommy's mocking grin when he called Ayesha "dark meat".

Okay, he and Tommy were on the same side, but sacrificing his knight to pin a king was a good exchange. The victory was what counted – betrayal just a necessary price.

To celebrate, he entered a caff and ordered a full English with a mug of strong tea. The bacon and the pork sausage were as sinful and delicious as vengeance. But he ate them quickly, lest anyone spy him.

For a joyful hour, Zami nursed his stratagem, shielding it like a burning ember to rekindle the fire. Then he realised the flaw. If he compromised Tommy, he would have to undermine himself too. He could only finger Tommy by confirming Rashid's accusation that he was a plant.

Triumph turned to despair.

Malachi wraps his wing around Zami, who sits bowed, his head in his hands. "Mum, why did you leave us? Dad, you created this clart so you could hide behind it. You cursed me with your darkness. You make me betray myself."

And Malachi laughs. The sound is like fingernails on a blackboard. "We always betray ourselves."

Betray yourself! It took Zami two days to realise this litany in his head was trying to help him, not taunt him. Of course! It was the only workable answer! The essence of a great lie is that as much of it as possible has to be true. To save himself, he needed to blow his cover.

Though he didn't know how to make a bomb, Zami knew all about spinning a story. He spent that week, until Friday prayers, crafting the legend. Then, after mosque, in the precinct, he put himself into Rashid's path.

"I don't have nothing to say to you, Zami," Rashid said.

"But I have something to say to you, brother Rashid, and you have to listen. It's important, right?"

Perhaps if Afaq hadn't been walking with his brother, he might have just shaken off Zami. It was Afaq who halted and asked, "What is it, brother?"

Zami made his eyes as luminously frank as he was able, his stance contrite, with head slightly lowered, only glancing up at the man. "You were right, brother Rashid," he whispered. "You were right. The filth were running me. I was an agent."

That made his quarry stop, mouth open in silent exclamation, beard quivering.

Zami raised his head, meeting Rashid's gaze. "I'm ashamed, brother. They had stuff on me, and they made me do it."

Rashid drew him to the side, away from the worshippers streaming from the mosque. "What stuff?"

Zami shrugged. "Drugs. I used to deal a bit, you get me?"

Rashid's lip curled.

"Not much and not now, not since I converted," Zami continued in a rush. "But they said they'd do me if I didn't help them."

Rashid folded his arms and settled his weight. "So, we was right to throw you out of the group. Come on, Afaq, let's go."

"Let him finish," Afaq begged and turned to Zami. "Why did they want you to get into the study group?"

"They think you're up to something. You're on a watch list, and I was your watcher."

Zami felt his heart flutter within his chest, like a bird. Now, now was the moment he needed the milky eye to turn.

"Rashid," he said, "there's something else. That's what I wanted to tell you. I'm ashamed and I had to warn you. They infected your computer with spyware. They're reading your e-mail and every file you open and every keystroke you make."

There! The sacrifice. The more savage the gods, the more they are gentled by sacrifice.

He can't remember when it happened. When his mother's smile started to fade, and she reached for a world he couldn't see. It was a lot for a child to take in, the first time he felt the chill of fear. They'll eat you up unless you sacrifice to them.

"That's impossible," Rashid said. "I run anti-virus and an anti-key-logger. I'd spot it."

He's asking you to prove yourself. And you can.

"Not this one. This one is from GCHQ."

"I don't believe you. I don't trust you, Zami. Prove it."

Use the truth. The truth is always the best shroud. You can win this. Be Zami. He has what Vince lacks.

The voice that spoke seemed to come from elsewhere, from far away. "I haven't seen the details. I'm just eyes and ears. They don't show me the logs. But they know about your weekend trips, where you go."

"Aldershot?" Afaq asked

Zami nodded. He felt a sudden flush of freedom.

"And Deepcut? Sandhurst?"

"Shut it," Rashid hissed to his brother.

Aldershot, Deepcut, Sandhurst – all military towns. So that was it!

Again Zami nodded.

"Shit!" Afaq exhaled, seeming to deflate. "It's true what he says. They're monitoring us."

"See, I was right not to trust the bastard," Rashid said.

Now they knew what he knew, and he knew they knew, but he was a step ahead – they didn't know what they didn't know.

"So if we can't trust him, why's he blabbing this?"

Rashid scowled. "How the fuck do I know? Maybe a double blind."

Zami kept a judicious silence.

"Or perhaps he's telling us because he's a mate and a good Muslim?" Afaq turned to Zami. "You're not lying to us, are you?"

"May Allah strike me dead if I lie. I'm going to be in deep shit with the filth when Rashid cleans his computer."

"What will you say?" Afaq asked.

"Not sure. I'll think of something."

"How about you tell them you had to confess to us, to curry favour?"

Zami stroked his beard. "I'd get a right bollicking for that, but yes it might work."

"Rashid, come on, he warned you. We owe him."

The silence that followed stretched into the forever. Both men watched as Rashid scowled, stroked his beard, frowned in thought, and finally smiled.

A trap? What did the smile mean? Had the man seen behind the mask?

"Would you be able to do something for us, brother Zami?"

"Anything."

"If we give you a story, can you report it back to the filth?"

Time was running out. He balanced on a knife edge, and it was exhilarating.

Zami chuckled. "It would be my pleasure. To stick it to them. I never asked to be their fucking secret agent."

Afaq grinned. "And now you can be a double agent."

Malachi is not impressed. He leans against a wall, cleaning his fingernails with a knife. "Where is your soul if the clart is a lie? Where is Ayesha? How will you save yourself?"

CHAPTER 20

"Maybe Zami could do some recon for us?" Afaq suggested.

Rashid frowned and shook his head.

"I mean, if they're got us under surveillance, you know?" Afaq continued. "But they won't be watching him, will they? It makes sense."

Rashid grabbed his brother by the shoulders and hissed, "Shut it!" jerking his head towards Zami.

Afaq brushed off the grip. "It's not like it's a secret now. He knows. The filth know."

Zami felt no tension. The scene receded and lacked personal connection with him. He folded his arms, watching the argument. He swivelled in curiosity from one man to the other, as if from the stands at a tennis match.

Afaq made to draw him in. "That's right, innit brother? They know?"

Zami tried to remember the answer. What was it they knew? A warm towel of muzziness wrapped his brain. But he understood he was rooting for Afaq, so he nodded his head.

"See?" Afaq pushed his face into Rashid's. "There ain't nothing to lose."

"I don't trust him. He's a snitch."

Afaq pleaded his case. But it would be Rashid who decided. The younger brother would always be the weaker party. He could propose, but the older brother would dispose. Afaq would fail.

"I don't think he's a snitch, or why let on about the surveillance?" Zami's champion argued.

Everything he said was a question rather than a statement. He needed Rashid's approval. The way to overwhelm the judge was not to ask but to pose incontrovertible arguments.

And Afaq seemed to hear Zami's thoughts.

"Even if he is a spy, we can still use him. He's not being watched. And he's white, so he can go places we can't."

Rashid stroked his beard.

Afaq shoulders squared, and he appeared to gain an inch in height. "We said, didn't we…?"

Tell, don't ask, Zami thought, urging Afaq on.

The man continued, "We said we'd stand out like sore thumbs in Sandhurst. But he can walk right in as if he belonged there. He does belong. He's one of them."

Zami wasn't sure which tribe he was part of. He belonged where he was put, blended with his surroundings. His loyalty lay with the part he was living out.

A bomb in the officers' mess, or on the parade ground. Could he do it? Where did the right lie? A bomb was bad. But regaining the brothers' trust was a good thing. It was of supreme importance. His mission was to gather evidence, and he didn't yet have enough.

Spin them out, play them like fish on the line. Give them room to run and then reel the whole lot in. He'd get a medal, for sure.

Rashid was still stroking his beard, the movement of his hand accelerating.

Afaq pressed his advantage. "The ceremony's next week, the Commandant's parade. We gotta decide, brother."

A parade? There would be trainee officers passing out, doting families, dignitaries. And lots of guns. That wasn't a lot like a harmless bang at the school toilets.

Perhaps the Queen would preside, taking the review. Should he just shop the brothers and the cell now? No, what he had on them wouldn't stand up in court. And Ayesha might never forgive him. But she already didn't forgive him. And she was considering shopping them. What to do?

Afaq was saying something, waving his hands about. Rashid was shaking his head and tugging at his beard. Zami hadn't heard what they said. He listened.

"… recon," Afaq said. "We can never get in there. Not if they're tracking us. They'll be watching all of us. But not Zami. He can…"

Recon! Not a bombing, just looking. Yes, he could look. There was no harm in that.

"Why would he tell us the truth?" Rashid asked.

"Because I hate them," Zami said. "I'll discover what you need to learn."

And he spoke the truth. He really hated them. The fury agitated his body. His hands shook. He felt revulsion. The bombs that had rained down on innocents, the troops that had scoured the holy lands with their army-issue boots, the rape of the oil, the cries of the women and children. He saw them all. He saw Tommy's sneering leer.

"Let me do this," he pleaded. "I can help."

Rashid examined him, eye-to-eye. He must have seen a *jihadi*'s righteous zeal there, because he nodded and stopped pulling at his beard.

The Commandant's display was the dress rehearsal for the Sovereign's parade. Were the brothers plotting something there at the high point of the officer cadets' year? That would be bold.

"What do you want me to do?" Zami asked.

Rashid pursed his lips. "Keep an eye out."

"Yes, but for what?"

Rashid crossed his arms. Evidently, he was still undecided about giving Zami any information, "Leave the planning to us," he said. "Just observe."

"I mean, I can't hardly wander around just keeping an eye out," Zami said "I need to be looking for something in particular, don't I? You have to tell me."

Afaq released a histrionic sigh. "Come on, bruv. He's right." He cocked his head, observing his brother. It looked like he didn't know exactly what the plan was either.

"Opportunities and barriers for an action," Rashid said after a long silence.

"Rashid, brother, I'm not a mind-reader," Zami said, his tone clipped.

Afaq seemed to see the irritation and tried to smooth matters over. "I think he means like where the sentries and lookouts are. Other ways in. Places things can be concealed."

"Also where the security cameras are, and whether they're fixed or mobile. Are there waste bins and, if so, where?" Rashid added.

Waste bins? Perhaps good places to leave a bomb. But he knew there would be no bins – too much of a security risk.

An image danced pretty in Zami's mind. A line of fireworks, each in its own bin along the edge of the parade ground, painting the sky with a fountain of silver, crackling to red and green fireflies and a final burst of golden sparkles.

Just a display, that wouldn't hurt anyone.

CHAPTER 21

The doorbell rang.

Zami's bones resonated with the sound. On the other side of the door, anything might be standing. Whatever lurked there, it was impatient: a fist hammered on the door. The concussion billowed the air.

"All right, coming," Zami shouted through the door, but made no move to open it. Instead, he studied the disturbance of the atmosphere. Not Ayesha, then: she didn't hammer so. Tommy might batter at the gate, but he didn't have the address. Or did he? And Tommy would by now have brought up siege engines of curses.

Malachi? Great leathery wings spread, pushing aside the dustbins and debris in the vestibule. Trampling the dandelions in the overgrown front yard, puffballs floating skywards like speech bubbles.

The air compressed as the door shook again, and Zami choked on the dense atmosphere expanding his lungs.

He opened the door.

It was nobody important. Just a delivery guy, with a potted bonsai tree on his trolley. He looked old, too old to be delivering anything as heavy as a tree.

"Where you want it?" the man asked, nodding his purple turban at the tree.

"I didn't order this," Zami said. "It's not for me."

The delivery guy showed him the address label. "Come on mate, time is running out."

Zami checked the label. "That's next door." He nodded his head at the low brick wall separating adjoining houses.

The delivery guy wore a purple turban, and sported jewelled rings on every finger. Where had Zami seen those before? "You're Adil, aren't you?"

The man didn't seem surprised to be recognised. He shrugged, wheeled the trolley into the centre of the little front yard, and tipped the thing, decanting the tree. A little mulch spilled onto old crisp packets and plastic drinks containers.

And then he was gone, leaving Zami to puzzle over the gift. He found no card, so he examined the miniature tree for clues. The tiny trunk and twisted branches were contorted as if with age. He was reminded of the olive trees of the Mediterranean, but the fruits of this tree hung heavy in green sacs, like ripening bananas. And the leaves had a polished gloss, adorning the tree like tiny mirrors.

He peered at a leaf and his reflected image stroked its beard back at him. A light drizzle began. When the water turned solid, he knew things were getting weird. Elongated raindrops hung from the branches like stretched taffy. He wondered if they might taste sweet. The air itself crystallised out and dropped in blue-white chunks from the sky, shattering musically on the ground.

So, it wasn't much of a surprise when a lamassu stepped into the yard, a winged beast with the head of a man and the body of a lion.

"Hello, lamassu," he said.

"Hello, man," the beast replied.

"What's happening?"

"You're having an episode."

"Oh, okay. I hope it doesn't stop. This is pretty."

The lamassu pawed the ground and tossed its head. "You can stay here as long as you choose."

"You're a figment of my imagination, right?"

"No."

"Oh. Well, I'm glad about that, in a way."

Zami was pretty sure lamassus weren't real. The animal seemed to read his mind. Zami could have sworn it smirked. Certainly, its nostrils flared in a snort. "In that case, how do you know I'm a lamassu?"

That was a stupid question. Everyone who'd ever seen Mesopotamian carvings recognised a lamassu. They adorned the gates of homes and palaces as protective icons.

The animal gave a patient sigh. "You're missing the point. There's a space in the bestiary, somewhere between men, lions and eagles, where a lamassu would exist, if it existed. And so, it does exist."

Underneath the bay window, crisp packets unfurled fleshy leaves, transforming into a bed of rhododendrons.

"The thing which doesn't exist," said the lamassu nodding its head toward the pot, "is that tree."

"It's as real as you are," said Zami.

"Yeah? So what's it called then?"

Zami reached, but the herbarium remained shuttered, and his fingers closed on no noun. The rain stopped, and he missed its moist caress on his cheek like a lover's tears. Sunlight lanced through the clouds, and a mirrored leaf flared.

"Mirrortree," he said.

"There ain't no such thing," said the lamassu, but turned its head to look, and Zami saw it had one milky eye.

He knelt and gave the tree an exhaustive examination. Up close, it was a tangle of bark and xylem, glossy wax and verdant chlorophyll. With his ear to one of the tiny pores through which the thing respired, he hoped it might whisper its name. A minuscule downdraft sucked at the fine hairs on his earlobes. But his ear remained empty.

Zami had an idea, but the idea stayed empty as a bell. The tree appeared familiar, rang a bell. Its emptiness created the sound of a struck bell. It *was* the sound, singing, whispering, insinuating the idea to him. But, for that idea, he had no name.

And, without names, there was no story. Anything could enter the tale.

And it did. The airs parted and, with a hiss of steam and a rumble of pinions, the exterminating angel occupied space. The voice rolled like thunder in the hills. "From the fruit of the tree of knowledge thou shalt not eat." Flame ran down the sword. Malachi was enjoying himself.

The lamassu cocked its head. "Oh? Why is that exactly?"

Malachi had an answer, but rendered in a language Zami did not speak, a guttural tongue full of clicks and hisses. The lamassu appeared unimpressed.

Zami asked, "So this is the tree of knowledge?"

"Yes," snarled Malachi.

"No." The lamassu tossed its head, great plaited beard swirling, and continued, "Knowledge is just a story, and the story doesn't exist until you tell it. Even then, it doesn't really exist until it's heard and takes up residence in the listener."

"Like a worm i' the bud," said Malachi. "It grows and grows, gnawing away from the inside. The story consumes truth."

At this, the lamassu capered round the yard, tossing its head in mirth. "The truth of a thing is only the story we tell about it. Take you for instance."

Then, it looked the demon tormentor full in the face, with an unwavering stare. "You're only a story he tells himself."

Malachi bellowed in anger and scythed his blade through the air. The heads of the rhododendron flowers tumbled, rolling in the dirt. Zami clutched at his neck, a line of red pain where the razor edge had caught him. But the fire on Malachi's sword dimmed and then was extinguished in a hiss of steam. Even his great bulk seemed to shrivel and thin. Through the armoured chest, Zami could make out the shape of the window bay behind.

Malachi tried to speak, but the sound was the emptiness of a bell being struck. Yet Zami knew what the great beast was trying to say.

"Behind it all, there is a truth."

And he felt the sense of it in his core. He understood Zami was a lie telling the truth, and Vince was a truth telling a lie.

Colours lost their vibrancy. The bushes shrivelled again to crisp packets and plastic bottles. The mirror tree inverted, burrowing into the litter, and was gone. The empty air closed with a small concussion around the dark angel and the winged lion. And Zami was once more alone.

CHAPTER 22

They might almost have been travelling in a Rolls Royce. People stopped and stared as they passed through the villages and towns of Surrey, heading towards the M3 motorway and Sandhurst military academy. This was no discreet car for a terrorist. But Rashid's Morris Traveller tickled Zami. There was something so quintessentially English about the classic vehicle, its polished bodywork in British racing green and its woodwork lovingly varnished.

At Lightwater, a man in a yellow cravat and a red Toyota Prius hooted his horn and gave them up a cheery thumbs up. Zami leaned forward from the back seat between the brothers.

"This old banger certainly gets you noticed," he said.

Rashid bridled. "Old banger? This is an icon, brother. They built cars to last in them days. The engine is bomb-proof."

Afaq giggled nervously, perhaps at the mention of bombs.

"I didn't mean no disrespect, brother," Zami said. "Yeah, they built proper cars then."

Rashid nodded, his tone smoother when he continued, suggesting he was mollified. "Everything in the old girl is functional, doing its job, nothing flashy. It's all simple. You're in control. Not like cars today. I maintain this myself, don't need no garage and computerised parts."

Zami understood the charm of being in control. "It's got personality, this car."

Perhaps too much personality, he thought. Why would a *jihadi* case a target in such a flamboyant and memorable car? Could be he was wrong. The brothers might just be posturing. Or perhaps it was a clever double bluff. Nobody would suspect someone who drew so much notice to themselves of being a terrorist.

"Personality, yeah," Rashid said. "That's it. You feel you're driving a real car, more in touch with the road."

"Doesn't it draw a lot of attention to you, though?" Zami asked.

Rashid laughed. "I'm six foot tall with a Muslim beard. Outside my own turf, how am I going to be inconspicuous anywhere, whatever model I own?"

"True that," Zami said.

Yes, maybe a cunning double bluff. Anyone driving such a car must be innocent.

As they entered the Lightwater slipway to the M3 and accelerated, Rashid pushed open the side window, tossing his head to let the breeze play with his long hair. Just like a road movie.

The estate car lumbered up towards seventy miles an hour, while indistinguishably aerodynamic modern cars whizzed past them. Rashid didn't seem to mind being overtaken.

"Had this old girl longer than my missus," he said.

They left the motorway at Frimley and headed north again in the Camberley direction. The perimeter of Sandhurst Academy was chain-link fenced and topped with concertina razor wire.

"Only way in is through the main gate," Afaq said.

"Unless you've got bolt cutters," Zami said.

Rashid sucked air through his teeth and pulled in to the little mosque on the London Road.

"Gate is about five hundred yards that way," he pointed east. "We'll wait here for you, where we won't draw any attention." He turned and handed Zami the ticket for the parade.

Afaq got out and tipped the passenger seat forward to let Zami squeeze past.

Trudging along the main road, Zami couldn't see the college fence, because a dense thicket of trees obscured it, but he felt its implacable presence. A roadside sign at the imposing entrance read "Commandant's Parade".

The guardhouse wasn't the usual drab sentry box and barrier. Instead, two sparkling white colonnaded gatehouses flanked the gate and ornate iron railings replaced the chain-link fence. The road passed between pillars. Zami sensed that on one side of this gate ran the easy life of possibility, while on the other was a world of order and discipline. There might be no going back if he punctured the membrane that separated the two.

He joined the line at the gate. Bag search, he noted as he watched others passing through. When his turn came, he showed his ticket to a guard in dress uniform. The inspection seemed to take ages, the squaddie scrutinising the document. Zami stood at parade rest, switching to an affected slouch when he thought this might look suspiciously formal. The guard looked up at him and down at the invitation again. What was wrong? A line had formed behind him. Had Rashid forged the ticket? Fucking idiot!

Malachi, leaning against the wall of the gatehouse, laughs. "Who's my little warrior, then?"

"Just follow the road straight ahead, sir," the guard said, handing the ticket back. "It will take you to the parade ground."

He followed a small group of others making their way up the drive. Most guests arrived by car, sweeping past them in Range Rovers, Mercs and Beamers. The driveway lay in the shadow of woods that pressed in on both sides of the road.

Plenty of places for concealment among the trees. A distant part of Zami's brain noted this and filed the information away.

A disputation consumed the foreground of his mind. He had to get back in the brothers' favour. A little bad thing might be all right if he could stop an even worse outrage.

Churchill had to let Coventry be bombed in the Second War so the Germans didn't discover we'd broken their code. Zami wondered whether this caused Winnie sleepless nights.

Whatever the philosophers said, in the real world, the choice wasn't usually between the good and the bad but between the bad and the worse. How did you work out, then, the right thing to do? Did you tot up the number of lives sacrificed and the number saved? Is that how Churchill made the decision?

Between the trees, shadows flitted and brief dappled shapes merged with the darkness. Possibly a deer or perhaps some much older creature.

But he didn't have to face Churchill's dilemma – no lives had to be lost. He could tip off the military police and they would clear the area. There'd just be a harmless little bang. Like the school toilets.

As far as he could tell, there were no surveillance cameras focussed on the driveway. You could hide a tank in these woods.

The trees began to thin and he glimpsed water. The roadway reached a bridge, crossing the stream, and the woodland fell back. To his left, a tranquil lake, and to his right beyond open lawns, the first buildings of the military academy, rising in red brick and white stucco against the horizon. The road intersected with another, and ahead of him was the Old College fronted by the parade ground.

A shiver of dread made him tremble. What was he doing here? What would Ayesha think?

On the tarmac, cadets' families and friends eddied and flowed. It was easy to blend into the crowd. Zami searched the space, but there were no waste bins or other places to conceal a device. And there were cameras.

The rehearsal began. Newly minted officers, fresh-faced and stern, turned, forming two lines moving in opposite directions. They drilled smartly in their black uniforms, with the red band on the trousers, their white belts and gloves. Some carried rifles, others swords. Zami could see nothing to indicate who got which weapon. They were all so young.

On the steps under a colonnaded portico, a band of what Zami believed might be Grenadier Guards played, in grey overcoats and tall black busbies. Eventually the marching stopped and all the cadets formed up facing the reviewing stand. There were speeches, but Zami heard nothing.

So young! But these babies will kill. Zami considered what had been done to the *Ummah* in Afghanistan, in the chaos of Libya, in the atrocities of Iraq. Defenceless mothers and children and old people bombed and blown up. Innocent youths rounded up, hooded, and tortured. If these baby officers died, would this not be fair retribution? He felt the certainties of his world fall away.

Earlier, he had considered Churchill's moral dilemma about Coventry. But this was the same Churchill who, as head of the War Office in 1920, had authorised gassing the Kurds during an uprising in Iraq. The great man had advocated a "lively terror", recognising that while chemical weapons were, of course, prohibited in conflict between civilised nations, this did not apply to wars with uncivilised nations and tribes. Rashid had told Zami this, and perhaps he had not lied. Zami's fists tightened at his side.

Malachi sneers, "You don't know any more what side you're on, do you, boy? You've lost yourself."

But he did know. He was on the side of the innocents, in Ayesha's camp.

The speeches had ended and the reviewing officer mounted his horse and rode slowly across the ceremonial space and up the steps and through the great doors of Old College. It was like some cowboy movie. Zami suppressed a snort of derision.

The military precision of the cadets' lines broke as they spilled out to join their families and supporters. Zami followed a straggle of visitors down the road to the way out.

Where was the right, he wondered? To report fully to Rashid and Afaq or to mislead them? Through the tree-lined drive and out the gate he wrestled with the dilemma. The college had vulnerabilities. But innocents might die. Yet, if he allowed these young officers to take the field, innocents would die anyway. Turning left he made his way back to Camberley mosque.

Nobody had died yet. Whatever operation the brothers were preparing wouldn't happen until the Sovereign's Parade. If he could learn what they planned he could foil it. Ayesha would want that. But to learn that, he needed to trade them information for trust.

By the time he reached the mosque, he'd decided.

As they drove back, he debriefed fully and with exactitude, described the bag searches, the cover of the trees, the lack of waste bins, and suggested that it might be easier to get into one of the public lectures Sandhurst held.

He waited for Rashid to reveal the plan. But the man just grunted, tightened his hands on the leather-covered steering wheel, and said, "You done good, brother. Thanks."

CHAPTER 23

Still no closer to knowing what the brothers planned, Zami took to hanging out near Ayesha's shop. Somehow he had to convince her he was true and loyal. Crossing the central precinct, he spotted the Cross of St George youths.

Footsteps closed in on him, and he heard a snuffling of respiration.

"Oi, traitor. I ain't done with you."

He looked about him. The narrow lane was deserted ahead, and all the doors were shut. So close to the shop, but not close enough. He turned to confront the fascists. They crouched, low and smiling.

The lad who'd barged him days ago in the plaza stalked near, the rest hanging back, watching. Zami adopted a boxer's stance.

"Oh, lovely," the thug said. "Queensberry Rules is it?" His companions guffawed, and he gave an acknowledging smile. "Proper little gentleman, ain't you?"

All he had to do was flash his warrant card. But he didn't carry the card undercover. Zami knew he was in for a beating, so a little bravado wouldn't add to the hurt. "If you believe you know the answers, why ask?"

It would happen soon. The lad closed on him, fists rising. And then a voice, Ayesha's voice.

"Stop that. Leave him alone." She put herself between the thugs and Zami.

"Look here. It's a letter box." The lad moved towards her with a leer. "I got something to post in your slot."

He reached to snatch away her hijab. "Open wide."

"What? Would you hit a woman?" Ayesha spoke coolly and without a tremor, contempt dripping from every syllable. "How brave!"

Zami pushed past. "Go," he hissed to her.

He lunged, grabbing the lad in a bear hug and trapping the arms. His biceps strained as his opponent stepped back and then a bony cranium slammed into his face. A fist drove into his stomach. And he was going down.

"Fucking traitor." A boot in the ribs.

Zami covered his head, protecting it as best he could, while heavy boots trampled and kicked.

"Stick up for your own people, not terrorists." A different voice. More boots.

"Paki-loving traitor."

"Traitor."

There was warmth on his face. Probably his nose where he'd been head-butted. And a brokenness in his side that stabbed when he inflated his chest.

"Tell your Paki bum boys we've got more of this for them. Tell them the streets are only for English patriots. Fuck off to Syria."

A sound of running feet. Everything went dim and far away. Someone kicked him in the balls, a sensation that must have been sharp agony and then endless aching. One last kick to his ribs and it stopped.

After a long, long time, gentle hands lifted him. He wasn't sure whose. A shoulder supported him. His own legs walked him, every step tearing at his ribs. But the kindness soothed his spirit. He looked to his side. The friend supporting him was Afaq. Tears ran down Zami's cheeks.

"Thank you," he murmured.

Afaq stared down at his trainers. "Weren't nothing. Not for a brother."

And Zami wept again.

Afaq passed him a tissue. "It's going to be alright. Let's get you cleaned up, mate. I think you're okay, but you got blood on your face."

Zami tried to paw at his cheek, where he felt the crusted gore, but lifting his arm jabbed blades of pain into his side.

Afaq led him to the family shop. Ayesha was nowhere in sight, and Zami was relieved she couldn't see him like this. It was her father behind the counter.

"What happen?" he asked.

"He's been attacked, *Abbu*," Afaq said. "Fascists probably. He's Muslim. He was protecting Ayesha."

"Take him upstairs."

Afaq shepherded him through the back store, up a narrow flight of stairs, and into a small sitting room crammed with overstuffed sofas. His saviour sat him on a sofa with bright red upholstery still in its plastic factory covers.

Afaq called to his mother, "Hi, *Ammi*. Just me. I've brought a friend. He's hurt."

But it was Ayesha who arrived. She stopped, hand to her mouth. "Oh, God, Zami."

Her brother left and Zami heard the sound of running water from the next room, followed by the creak of cupboards opening and closing.

"What have they done to you? I ran to get Afaq as fast as I could." Ayesha said.

"I'll live. I've had worse," Zami said and tried to laugh, but the jerk to his torso harvested agony again.

Afaq returned with a bowl of water, a cloth and a bottle of antiseptic. Pushing Ayesha aside, he knelt and began to clean the blood from Zami's face. Zami hissed in pain.

"Gently," Ayesha said, "You're hurting him. Get out of the way and let me do that."

With tender care, she cleaned his face. It hurt, but he tried not to show it. He didn't want her to stop.

"Take your shirt off, Zami," she ordered.

"No," Afaq said. "It's not right."

"Don't be such an idiot, Afaq. He's injured. I need to see how badly."

Her brother folded his arms and frowned. "Alright, but not the trousers."

Her fingers fumbled as she undid the buttons. Probably, Zami thought, this was distress, since she'd grown quite adept at undressing him, but maybe the clumsiness was a show for Afaq. If so, the acting skill was unexpected and impressive.

She eased the shirt off, wincing when he did. "Sorry, sorry," she kept saying.

Fingers whose caress he knew well touched, inspected, probed. He wanted to lean in and kiss her. She gave the slightest shake of her head and smiled. The whole world was in that smile. He acknowledged their secret with a near-imperceptible nod. It was all going to be okay.

"I don't think anything's broken," she said. Her hand lingered on his chest, eyes bright with tears, and the hairs on his arm stood up. "But you're going to have the mother of all bruises. Poor, poor Zami."

Afaq appeared startled and then raised an eyebrow. Ayesha looked down and withdrew her hand from Zami's chest. But he believed he still had her love, that he was forgiven.

"What is he doing here? What's going on?" Rashid was in the room and he was not happy.

CHAPTER 24

"Tell me a story," Ayesha said. "Another one about Don Vincent and his Ayesha."

Zami had healed quickly. Ayesha's love for him, likewise. There was scarcely a bruise left on either his body or his romance four days after the crisis. A&E, to which Rashid had insisted he be taken, had discharged him the same day, with cold packs and a prescription for painkillers.

Now Zami cradled Ayesha in his arms, the sweat of their lovemaking cooling on skin as he stroked her belly. Of course, her accusation still stood. But it was, for the moment, subsumed.

"You are as hungry for tales as you are for pleasure, *habibti*," he teased.

"Those aren't different things," she said, moving slow and powerful like the tide under his touch. "You tell me stories with your body and with your mouth. Both fire my imagination."

"Okay, I'll use my mouth." He grinned and shuffled down her body to where his hand rested.

She giggled and pushed his head from between her thighs. "Mind you use it to tell me of Don Vincent. I've come too much. I think I'd break if you took me again."

He pretended to pout.

"You look like a fish," she teased.

He exhaled a long breath of air. "All right. Don Vincent it shall be. I will give you the tale of how Ayesha saved him."

The armies of Ferdinand and Isabella, the Catholic Kings, were close now. Málaga, Granada's last port, had fallen to them. The citadel had been a formidable obstacle to the enemy.

Málaga's defenders rained down arrows, stones and boiling pitch on the Christians in the plain below. Ferdinand brought up his terrible cannon, the "Seven Sisters of Ximines", which wrapped the fortress in smoke and flame day and night. Some of the ramparts were blown with mines. But still the citadel held out. The chivalry of Catholic Spain was now gathered about the walls of Málaga, and Isabella herself arrived, giving new heart to the besiegers. But none of Ferdinand's weapons felled the city. It was famine that did it. Málaga surrendered.

King Boabdil of Granada, known as Ez-Zogoiby – "the Unlucky" – had seen the threat too late. Captured by the Catholics, he had been turned and used the alliance to defeat his rivals. Only when Málaga was lost, cutting his supply routes; only when Ferdinand and Isabella ranged the fertile plains beyond his city, with forty thousand foot and ten thousand horse; only then did he take up arms against them.

Sad songs and bitter stories filled Granada's plazas.

"Time is running out," called old Adil, still hawking magic phials from his stall in the alley. Many other traders were gone, the donkey trains no longer winding their way into the Al-bayyazin laden with wares from far off lands. Gone too were the woven silks, delicate glassware from Almeria, and the iridescent majolica pots from the Balearics.

"Time is running out."

Don Vincent laughed. "You say that every day, my friend."

The merchant waved a hand, light flashing from his jewelled rings. "And is it not true every day, señor?"

"I suppose it must be. Every day we come closer to our end."

"And yet you age not," Adil said. "What is your secret?"

"Love, my friend. Love."

For he adored Ayesha, and she him, and together they linked arms against the threats surrounding Granada.

In the plaza, Don Vincent declaimed to his audience: "Beautiful Granada! The soft note of the lute no longer floats through thy moonlit streets, and the serenade is no more heard beneath thy balconies; the lively castanet is silent upon thy hills. Orange and myrtle still breathe their perfumes into the Alhambra's silken chambers; the nightingale still sings within its groves. Alas! The countenance of the king no longer shines within these halls."

"Traitor!" one listener cried, and then another and another. "You are not truly a Muslim. When the Catholic armies arrive, you will turn your coat. They will save you as a Christian, while they slaughter us or carry us off into slavery, as they did the folk of Málaga."

Don Vincent saw the night watchman, Tomaz, slink away into the safety a dark alley. A Christian for sure.

The mood grew ugly. Don Vincent ran, not stopping to pick up his hat with its thin scattering of coins.

"We can kill ourselves one Christian at least," a voice shouted, "before they murder us all."

A thunder of feet echoed behind him in the narrow alleyways as he twisted and turned through the maze, seeking to throw them off. He burst through the gate of the Al-bayyazin and onto the esplanade by the River Darro. Still the mob pursued him, closer now, and he was tiring.

Just when all seemed lost, a voice rang out, stern and implacable. "Stop that. Leave him alone."

Ayesha, returning from her duties at the Alhambra Palace, put herself between Don Vincent and the pursuers. She was fearless as Khawla Bint al-Azwar, charging the Christian army at Damascus to rescue her brother.

A man stepped forward, his fist bunched and the veins bulging at his temple.

"What? Would you strike a woman?" Ayesha spoke coolly and without a tremor, contempt dripping from every syllable. "How brave have the people of Granada become! They fight women and their own brothers because they quake before the Christians! Oh Granada, for shame, for shame."

Her assailant backed away, shaking his head. "That man is a Christian, a spy. He will betray us."

"That man," Ayesha said, "is a Muslim and my husband. Allah gave him to me, and you will not take him, or harm him. You all know him as a good man. Is this what your fear has made you become? For shame, Granada! Pity Al Andalus!"

Before her fury and her contempt, the crowd grew sheepish. They looked at the cobbles, none daring to meet her glare.

"If you are so eager to fight and kill," she said, "the city gates are there. Go and find yourself Islam's enemies where they burn the fields and ravage our villages. Battle them, but not our own. Granada has need of heroes today."

The men drifted away, back to their meagre shops and diminished ateliers.

"Time is running out," Adil whispered in Don Vincent's ear, "but it seems you still have luck with which to purchase more."

Ayesha's brothers, too, feared time was running out. They urged Don Vincent to recast the story.

"Turn the infidel armies away from us," they pleaded. "Let them rather pivot east, against France."

And he told them such a tale, blinding the Catholic Kings to Granada.

"Perhaps," he suggested, "if I think not on their Majesties, they will cease to exist."

"And thus did Ayesha save Don Vincent," Zami finished.

"As I would save you," she said. "Frail woman though I am."

"As you did save me," he said. "You're the strongest person I know. Rashid trusts me again, I think. What you said to him must have worked."

But Zami realised it wasn't Ayesha's pleading that had done the trick. He knew the true price at which that trust had been bought.

CHAPTER 25

Only with Ayesha could he find peace.

"Once upon a time…" Zami began.

Ayesha, snuggling against him in his flat, said, "And they all lived happily ever after."

That was Ayesha all over – she liked endings, while Zami favoured beginnings. While she craved certainty, he preferred ambiguous possibility.

"You have to let a story unfold," he said. "Give it space to breathe."

Ayesha shook her head, tendrils of her hair drifting across his neck and shoulders like grasses in the wind. The iron tang of her scent blew across him. "Stories are events in the light of their endings," she said.

He had heard this before. She believed that, while life is lived forwards, stories must start at their climax and be written backwards.

"Do you realise," she said, "that in the original version of *Sleeping Beauty*, she doesn't wake up when the Prince kisses her?"

"No, I hadn't heard that."

"Nor does she wake up when he rapes her. She wakes nine months later giving birth to twins."

That finale certainly changed the tale. Zami wondered how their ending would change their story, but kept his counsel. Ayesha was in a playful mood, and he liked the unexpected places that often led.

"How about," he said, "if Jack doesn't climb back down the beanstalk with the hen and the golden eggs, but instead they arrest him for housebreaking?"

She pumped her fist. "Rights for ogres. I like that. Tell me another story, an alternative fairy tale, with a different ending."

"Not about Don Vincent and Ayesha? Okay. Let me see, once upon a time there was a little wooden puppet."

Ayesha took his hand and kissed it. "I know this one."

"No, you don't. Shh. The little wooden puppet looked like a boy, but he had a wooden head and a wooden heart. He was so sad when he saw the children pass by the toy shop, but none of them ever lifted him down from his top shelf and took him home to play. In all the world, the thing he most wanted was to be a real little boy."

Ayesha bit the heel of his thumb playfully. "I have so heard this tale."

"No, wait, *habibti,* listen. The little wooden puppet was sad and lonely on his perch. One winter's night, he stared out through the frosted window at the dark sky beyond. And he saw a light. It got closer and closer until the glow filled the gloomy toy shop and into the room flew a sparkling fairy godmother.

"'Why so sad, little puppet?' she asked.

"'I want to be a little boy,' he said.

"The fairy raised her wand. There was a bang and a flash and a cloud of smoke. When the haze cleared, there on the top shelf where the little puppet had been, was a pile of charred wood."

Ayesha laughed and punched his chest. "That's awful."

"You hadn't heard it before, though, had you?"

"*Alhamdulillah*, no."

As the day ended, and the darkness climbed on the windowpane, they played with endings. Each finale was more fanciful than the last, moving from fairy tales, to films, to classic novels.

"How does our story end, Zami?" she asked.

"Happily ever after, I hope."

"They sailed off into the sunset?"

Sunsets always made him sad. He'd looked it up once and discovered it was a known condition, Hesperian depression. "Or maybe into the dawn?"

"That sounds like the start of another tale," she said. "But then the best endings are also beginnings."

Zami, pretending to be sapped by their earlier lovemaking, rolled off the sofa onto his hands and knees. "You want coffee?" he asked, crawling towards the kitchen alcove.

Ayesha laughed, and the laugh pleased him. "Yes please, if I haven't finished you off, and then I want you to make us a new ending."

To her mirth and delight, he groaned and levered himself up on the worktop. Passing a hand over his fevered brow, he filled the water jug of the espresso machine, then spooned coffee into the filter handle and tamped it down, pantomiming exhaustion. When the apparatus began to give off satisfying gurgles, Zami turned and laughed.

"I think I might just survive, but it'll be a near thing. A new ending? Woman, you're insatiable."

"You're an animal. I meant for our story, silly."

He carried the two little cups over to her. "What would you like to change about us now?"

She thought for a moment, head cocked. A ray of light from the streetlamp lanced through the grimy window and licked her cheek. "I hate this sneaking around. If Rashid and Afaq would only accept us, we could be together openly. That's how I'd rewrite the story."

"So," Zami said, "I'm accepted into the family, and it all goes smoothly?"

"Yes. And I go to university and become a literature scholar." She laughed. "Happily ever after."

"Or, perhaps we run away to sea and sail into the sunset," Zami suggested.

"Oh yes, much more romantic, a much better yarn. We could live, happy and penniless on a desert island, surviving on fish and coconut milk."

Then it was Ayesha's turn again to devise an ending.

"Perhaps," she said, "we have to give up some time, to gain luck, you remember, like Don Vincent and his stallholders?"

"That would create a very classical ending. An exquisite and tragic death together."

"That's how a love like ours is. Think Romeo and Juliet, Tristan and Isolde, Shirin and Khosrow."

Zami had a vague idea of the story of Tristan and Isolde but did not know the ancient Persian tale of Shirin and Khosrow. Ayesha delighted in reciting it.

"Romantic love is incompatible with earthly life, and its proper end is death," she said, when she'd done.

Zami scratched his head. "Then we must try to be unromantically in love."

CHAPTER 26

Zami believed he remembered a lunch. Perhaps, it happened on the banks of the Thames, or maybe the Tigris, he couldn't be certain. Anyhow, on the upper terraces of some brushed concrete neo-brutalist ziggurat. Was the location named The Hanging Garden?

He was pretty sure the diners included himself, Tommy, and Ishtar. Veils obscured the recall of what had brought them together. He sensed the shape of it, the feel, but, as if it were a rainbow, it didn't stay in place long enough to catch hold of. It melted on the tongue.

Ishtar had licked her fingers, he remembered clearly, and then said, "Being loved."

Of course. What was the point of being a goddess without adoring believers?

The question they debated was what success meant. That, he recollected.

He also recalled Tommy had ordered the all-day breakfast, a full English. Zami had thought it common, the way the man mashed the baked beans on the concave surface of the fork. He had a clear picture too of Tommy eating hash browns from the flat of his knife, but that may have been in the Hendon canteen.

What he and Ishtar ordered, he was less sure. She probably had the whole spitted lamb, from her habit of licking her fingers. He rather fancied he'd had Imam Bayeldi. A spindrift memory of aubergine and toasted pine nuts lingered.

Tommy laughed with contempt at the idea that success entailed being loved. He held his belly as he chortled. The mirth looked staged.

"It's beating them down, the bad guys," he said.

Whether the guys were good or bad was largely irrelevant to Tommy, or so it seemed to Zami. Just so long as he could beat someone down. At Police College, the guy had been obsessed with the fact that if you hit someone exactly on the spine with your truncheon, the skin parted on both sides of the blow. But, Tommy being a copper, the opposition tended to be the bad guys. This was in the days before the extendible ASP friction lock baton replaced rubber truncheons.

Ishtar smiled at Zami over the top of the haunch she was chewing. "What is success for you, dear?"

"Being believed," he said without hesitation.

That made Tommy laugh again. "You're a fair liar, Vince me old mate. I'll give you that."

That was why Tommy was no good undercover. He understood only lies, not the craft that went into wearing a legend. With weary patience, Zami explained, "You are mistaken. Just because something didn't happen, doesn't make it untrue."

Ishtar chuckled and clapped her hands. "Well said. You may not be loveable, but at least you're interesting."

Zami remained immobile while the ice of that cruel compliment melted. Had he moved, he knew the shards would have sheared his heart.

To assuage the wound, he discussed old cases with Tommy. They reminisced about "The Woman", protagonist of the scandal of the compromising photograph and the Bohemian Arch Duke.

"The only woman who ever bested me," Zami noted.

He had then been playing the part of an Anglican cleric. Feigning injury in a brawl, he blagged his way into The Woman's house. She was kind, solicitous. He claimed to be feeling faint and asked if he might open the window. At his signal, Tommy threw in a smoke bomb, and Zami shouted "Fire!"

"I knew," he said, "she would instinctively rescue her most valuable possession. And so she did. She made immediately for a sliding panel and withdrew the photograph."

"Should have snatched the thing then and there," Tommy mocked. "That was your mistake. You screwed up."

"Well, I couldn't hardly, could I? Her boyfriend was there. It would have been indelicate."

As soon as she went for the panel, she understood what was afoot. The look she shot Zami was a mixture of chagrin and respect. Frustratingly, she had fled by the time Zami, Tommy, and the Archduke returned the next day. In the recess behind the panel was a letter addressed to Zami. In a firm, slanted script The Woman wrote that she had removed the photograph as insurance but that she had no intention of using it. She had found a better match. As a memento, she had enclosed a portrait of herself.

"What a woman," the Archduke sighed. "She would have made an admirable Queen. If only we were of the same station."

Zami had agreed they were indeed on different levels. He still treasured her picture.

"Speaking of women, are you still seeing that slapper?" Tommy asked. "What was her name? Ayesha?"

Ishtar banged the table, and the echo rumbled in the hills. "My boy doesn't go with slappers."

Bless her!

Zami clicked his tongue. "Ayesha hasn't happened yet, Tommy. She's a long way in the future. You know that."

Tommy's face took on the appearance of a wrung washcloth, rumpled and squeezed. His mouth opened soundlessly and then closed again. Zami wondered what the problem might be, Tommy's disquiet was beguiling and he watched in amused silence.

Ishtar gnawed her bone.

"What do you mean, hasn't happened yet?" Tommy finally spluttered, spraying hash brown over the dishes. Ishtar made a moue of disgust.

"What it usually means. It's in the future. Right? Stop playing silly buggers. This village already has more than its share of idiots."

The table lurched as Tommy half rose, fists balled. Other diners stopped eating and stared. *What the hell was wrong with the fuckwit?*

Ishtar swivelled to the crowd, hurling the gnawed bone at the nearest diner. "Nothing to see here." They quailed before her ire and burrowed back into their lives. She unleashed a beatific grin at Tommy, who sank into his chair.

"He's right, though," she said to Zami. "It makes no sense. Unless you've suddenly become a seer?"

Or at least he remembered words something like that. He seemed to recall her holding forth at length about time's arrow. And Tommy gratefully siding with her. The man was drawn to power, sucking up to his seniors.

Sycophant. Psycho-fancy. As Tommy flattered the warrior queen, Zami drew further away. Had the two of them concocted this as some game? Ayesha lay in the future. It was obvious. He could see her faintly if he strained. There she was, a tiny figure dancing across the plains of what is to come. They must be able to spot her too. Surely.

"Nobody can perceive the future," Ishtar said.

Years later, Zami encountered what economists call the "curse of knowledge". When you know something, it's hard to put yourself into the mindset of someone who lacks this information. But, at that time, he just understood her as wilfully obtuse.

Zami shook his head once in utter frustration. "I don't believe you."

Ishtar's eyes went wide, then narrowed. Much more dangerous than Tommy's pugilism. Tumorous clouds rolled in from the north, dark and veined by lightning. "Say that again," she demanded.

"I don't believe you."

And Ishtar grew sad and pale. "You're killing me," she whispered. What was the point of being a goddess without belief? Her flesh grew translucent until he saw the blue veins clearly, pulsing slow under the integument. Bit by bit, as the afternoon sun arced over the river, she shrivelled, disappearing into her leather armour.

"You're killing me," she said again, and her voice grew softer than the breeze agitating the decorative palms.

"I didn't mean it," Zami whimpered. "Please. Don't leave me."

That, he remembered sharply – speaking those words, and the sense of loss, the desolation. And the empty leather breastplate.

CHAPTER 27

"Oi." There was no mistaking the shouter, nor his anger.
Zami turned and snarled, "Fuck off, Tommy."

Tommy pushed his nose right up to Zami's, his breath a foul blend of halitosis and cigarettes. "No, Vince, I'm done fucking off. You're in deep shit."

The crust of the world cracks and Zami glimpses the realm beneath. Malachi's mouth opens, his voice sepulchral, "They're here. They see you."

Zami smells the stench of decay and tumbles in. Past the gnashing teeth and into the gullet. The walls tighten, squeezing him like a fat white worm wriggling through the earth. In the constriction, it's hard to breathe.

"Someone will see you, idiot," Zami warns.

"Vince, I'm really past sodding caring. What did you do?"

In the darkness of the tunnel, Zami senses a presence. Malachi is here. "What did you do, boy? You've got a beating coming." Malachi is inside himself.

"Nothing. What you talking about?"

Tommy rocked on the balls of his feet from one leg to another, like a boxer blocking his exit. "Then how come

Rashid has found the spyware on his computer and deleted it?"

There is a world inside and a world outside. And, in each, he faces an adversary. Zami leaves Vince to deal with Malachi and answers Tommy.

Vince laces his fingers in a star, calling on Ishtar. "Mum, why did you abandon us?" Ishtar doesn't respond.

"Tommy, you moron, he's an IT graduate. Now get lost before someone sees us together and you blow it."

But Tommy wasn't having any of it. He just stood there, shaking his head. Zami spun on his heel and started to walk away. Meaty fingers grabbed his arm, and he almost slipped.

"Where do you think you're going, you little arsehole? I'm not done with you. If you want me to give you a little tap, I'm happy to oblige." Tommy raised his free hand, balled into a fist.

Tommy had never hit him before. They'd come close once in the canteen, but never scrapped. There was anger in the man's eyes, but also excitement. Tommy wanted to hurt him, needed him to offer an excuse.

Zami shrugged. "Work it out, Tommy. What would I have to gain by telling Rashid?"

"How the fuck do I know? You're a weird little tosser. Always have been. Who gets why you do what you do? My guess is, you've gone bush. That Paki tart has turned your head. Maybe I should have a word with Rashid and Afaq and tell them what you're up to with their sister."

The walls of the underworld pulse, shunting Vince towards the acid pit in its stomach. "Ishtar," he cries, "save us". No help comes. Ishtar is sulking. Above ground, Zami secretes walls, repairs the floor to give himself foothold. Malachi doesn't belong in his story. He faces Tommy.

Don't lash out. Don't rise to it. It's what he wants. Take control.

Zami bottled up his anger and terror, turning them into a sigh. "Yeah, Tommy, that makes a lot of sense. I've gone over to the dark side. That's why I told you about the bases."

"Huh? What bases?"

"In my last report, Tommy. It was only the day before yesterday, you remember?"

Tommy shoved his face close again, his contempt flecking Zami's cheek with spittle. "What report, you lying bastard? The bin was empty."

"Then the bin men got to it before you, didn't they, you lazy shit?"

"Dog ate your homework, eh? I don't believe you, Vince."

Only the truth was going to suffice. Zami filled the gaps between each slowly articulated word with patient contempt. "Rashid and Afaq are visiting military bases. On their weekend jaunts. Aldershot, Deepcut, Sandhurst."

Tommy whistled. "Well bugger me gently. Scoping out targets, you think?"

"Possibly."

Ishtar races in, scarf billowing, sword drawn. Just as she scattered the enemy at Damascus, so now she flies to Zami's aid. "He doesn't see you now. Clever, clever. In the murk, anything can hide."

"I've got this. Help Vince," Zami shouts.

Zami stared at Tommy, unblinking. "Are we done, now? Are you going to piss off and stop risking my cover?"

Tommy looked sulky and dipped his head in grudging agreement.

"And are you going to check the drop for messages in good time? Or there's not really much point in me writing the sodding reports, is there?"

"Fuck you, Vince."

Zami gave a genial nod. "Fuck you, Tommy. Run along now, there's a good lad."

As Tommy trundled away, Zami let out a hiss.

Deep in the underworld, Malachi laughs. He knows what's coming. Vince stares about, helpless. It's like crossing into another world, where everything looks the same, but feels different – an imposter world. He senses the walls pulsing, digesting him, fingers probing, searching for secrets inside of him – secrets even he doesn't grasp. And then Ishtar is there. "Expand your chest," she says. "Breathe." But the walls are so tight.

"What did you mean, like, 'check the drop for messages'?" Rashid detached himself from the shadow of a nearby doorway.

"And why did he call you Vince?" Afaq joined his brother.

It reminded Zami of that time when he was in a crash, and the car rolled arse-over-tip all the way down the hill. Everything went slow, sounds deadened. Even the adrenaline flow meandered sluggish to the coast.

Ishtar gifts Zami time. She summons Crow, who turns his milky eye.

He had time to flip through all the options, like a deck of cards. Without any idea how long the brothers had been there, or what they'd heard, best stick to the truth. And let them tell him how much they knew. With luck, they'd missed most of it.

"That was the filth," he answered, and his voice sounded muffled by great distance. "His name's Tommy, and he's my handler. They made me work for them. I have to leave messages for him in a dead drop. And Vince is the name he knows me by. It was my name before I converted, wasn't it?"

"You seemed very matey," Rashid said. His tone was accusatory.

"Did we? You can't have been watching too hard. We hate each other."

"So you wouldn't mind if he had a little accident, yeah?" Rashid asked.

Afaq stood to the side, hands on his hips.

A test! That had to be a test. If he warned Tommy, they'd know not to trust him. Zami grinned. Tommy would have to take one for the team.

"Quite the reverse, I'd be made up," he said. "Kick his head in."

Rashid watched him in silence, arms folded, lips pursed.

Zami smiled his most disarming grin. "I mean it. Tommy's made my life a misery. You'd be doing me a favour if you did him over."

"Oh yeah," Rashid nodded. "That I believe. What I can't figure out is whose side you're really on. I still don't trust you."

Ishtar cuts and slashes with her scimitar, paring the walls, letting him breathe.

"Well, what can I do to convince you? How about that story you wanted me to relay to the filth? Did you decide on one yet?"

Rashid stroked his beard. "What story do you suggest?"

"I couldn't say. An interest in regimental history, perhaps? All depends on why you were visiting those towns, really."

"Exactly that, brother Zami, an interest in regimental history."

He's nearly there. The walls are paper thin now. He could put his fist through them, and break into other tunnels, other stories. Except, his fist is suddenly made of glass. "Take care," Ishtar says. "Take extreme care, or you'll shatter."

CHAPTER 28

Vince sat alone in the little flat, holding himself tight. The sun dipped low beyond his window. Every now and again, his body tremored, as if magma were pushing against his crust. Volcanic dread circled his walls. Soon those ramparts would be breached. All his stories lay in bits, bombarded by Tommy and Rashid's siege engines. But it was the breaking of Ayesha's trust that forced the rupture. He had fought for his dreams but there was no way to win; he ran from the murk but it only brought him nearer, and he led it to her.

A cup of coffee stood on the table – undrunk, cold. Vince stared at it, trying to understand what it was. Everything familiar had turned alien. And he heard the clash of shields beyond his stockades.

"Cup," he said, remembering the word meant something, but unable to tell what that meaning might be. His words had abandoned him, circling above his head like the strange and fascinating toys hung from an infant's crib.

He would tell no more stories. Only the tongue of his inner world retained meaning.

Squeeze. He knew that word.

The walls closed tight around him and pulsed in slow peristalsis. They were digesting him, each rhythmic squeeze moving him towards the great pool of acid that waited in the stomach of the world.

Even the gods he worshipped could die and be replaced.

Crow taunts. "To these gods you cannot pray. They will break you."

The squeezing was Tommy. And Rashid was the lake of acid in which he would dissolve. His surface billowed, and he became ovoid, attempting to offer the least resistance to the crushing forces that moved him on.

Ayesha. His poor Ayesha. She was in danger. And he was helpless. He had no choice.

The words of a song came to him. "Humpty Dumpty sat on a wall."

And Crow offers a mocking echo. "Un petit d'un petit s'etonne aux Halles."

His eggshell fragility might shatter so easily into a million sharp fragments. The secret lay in keeping himself still and whole.

A beginning, middle, and end. He was a story. If he succeeded in hanging onto his middle, his now, he might find his way back to his beginnings. Provided he could keep Crow's milky eye turned towards him.

"Dad, you created this murk in order to hide behind it. You cursed me with your darkness. Mum, why did you leave us?"

Crow laughs. "They won't answer you. You're alone. You've always been alone."

"No, not alone. I am loved."

"You betrayed your duty in search of love. You betrayed your family. You betray your love too because you are weak."

"That's just a story. There are other endings. And I know you lied. You appear as Crow, but I recognise you, Malachi."

Malachi spreads his wings, with a terrible leathery crackle, like the flick of a bullwhip. "Where did you honestly think this story would end? How else can it end but in failure and betrayal?"

"I am Zami."

"You are Vince. And Vince is weak."

"I am who I choose to be. Zami is strong, people like him, people trust him."

"Rashid doesn't trust him. Tommy doesn't trust him. He's a lying shit."

Zami reached for his coffee, pondering what a lie might mean.

How delightfully simple the world would be if telling the truth was always right, and lying was always wrong. Social life is lubricated by what people call white lies, which shield the other person from damaging truths.

Zami constructed a natural history of lies, telling each one off on a finger.

Lies that harm, and help no-one;
Lies that harm some, and help others;
Lies told for the pleasure of lying;
Lies told to please others in smooth discourse;
Lies that harm no-one and help others materially;
Lies that harm no-one and help others spiritually;
Lies that harm no-one and protect others.

St. Augustine, he seemed to remember, believed all these lies to be sinful, but in descending order of severity. Muslims recognised the *toriya*, a falsehood created without telling a lie. It is permissible for a Muslim to offer a *toriya*, or even an outright lie, to unbelievers if it is necessary to avoid a risk of harm.

If Zami had lied, this fell into the category of Noble Lies, those told to protect others, to preserve law and order. It was said these porkies harmed no-one, but he wasn't sure. Though they may have been told with love, they corrupted other loves.

But a lie was only a story, one among many. Stories tell us what goes with what, what is important and what is unimportant, who to praise and who to blame. Facts are everything that is the case, stories are the connections between them.

Tommy was to blame. And he deserved the kicking that was coming his way. Zami was a wandering troubadour who had won the love of the maiden. She led him to the hidden tower and the pot of gold. But he had eaten the fruit, and the gold had vanished.

No. Someone else ate the fruit. The fasting priest. Maybe, Tommy. It was Tommy's fault. Zami had given up Tommy and now Rashid would love him again. But how could Ayesha love him again? The moment of betrayal is always agonising. To betray something you must first love it.

In the darkness a light glimmers and grows. It comes from within the armour itself and spills out behind her like the trail of a comet. "Excellent," Ishtar says. "Why suffer the past when there's a new road ahead? The world is collapsing. Fine, let it collapse. Raze the world to the ground. Only then, as a newborn, can you see everything afresh. Find your purpose!"

"Dad, I'm leaving. It's for the best."

Ishtar's voice is soft as a lullaby. "A life without loss is a life without love. Let go of the fear."

Malachi snarls. "He can't. He needs his fear. Because he's weak."

Ishtar's demurs. "Yes, he can. We will help him. We're always there to help him."

Vince's voice was strangled and faint. "This is where my story began, with a fabrication and this is where it must end. Because I can't see any further. It now becomes someone else's legend to tell."

Vince fell through the mesh of the world. He understood he was somewhere else. It was quiet, so very quiet. He had nothing left. No fear, no hate, no quest. Nothing. The voices fell silent. And they had no power over him. He let the threads of his legend drift away on the current as he was carried gently to a place the darkness couldn't reach.

The waves lapped on the shore, ebbing and returning. The world is always there, waiting to be described.

CHAPTER 29

Just the day before, Ayesha had come to him in the flat, fear in her eyes. "Zami, I'm pregnant."

He said the usual silly things men say – What? How? Why? Are you sure?

"It will be all right, won't it?" she asked. "You must marry me."

He played for time. "Your brothers will never allow it."

"My brothers and father will kill me if I have a baby and I'm unmarried."

Stories fanned out ahead of him. There was the one in which they married and triumphed over adversity and prejudice. And another in which she died, leaving him to mourn with tragic grace. Neither sufficed. Neither led to the exposure of the plot, Ayesha's safety, and his commendation. Perhaps, if Rashid and Afaq could be jailed, she would be safe. But would his evidence stand up in court? The pregnancy was the one fact he couldn't narrate away.

"*Habibti*, you must get rid of it."

"I will not."

The moment of betrayal is always agonising.

***

Of all the stories he'd recounted to her about Don Vincent, he had ever kept the final one untold.

The chivalry of Catholic Spain was drawn up under the walls of Granada. Nothing passed in or out of the city – no food in, no refugees out. The seven-hundred-year splendour of Al Andalus formed a beacon of art and learning, stretching from Zaragosa in the north to Algeciras in the south, from Lisbon on the Atlantic to Valencia on the Mediterranean. Cordoba had been the greatest city in Europe, attracting scholars and merchants, sculptors and architects, just as diminished Granada had drawn Don Vincent to the last flicker of the torch. Now the Emir Boabdil gazed out from the windows of the Alhambra Palace and saw only desolation.

"It is not for nothing," Boabdil's mother said, "that they call you Ez Zogoiby, the unlucky."

"It was written in the book of fate," he replied, "that I should be unlucky, and the kingdom should come to an end under my rule."

Boabdil strode the halls and chambers of the palace that had become his prison. So foolish! He believed he could use the Catholic Kings, Ferdinand and Isabella, to aid him in his struggle with his father and then his uncle. But they had used him. Ferdinand confided to an ally, "To put Granada in division and destroy it, We have decided to free him. He has to make war on his father."

Boabdil did nothing as the Catholic Kings took territory after territory from his uncle. Only after he helped the Christians take Málaga, did Boabdil understand what was coming and rebel. Too late, much too late. In 1491, an army of forty thousand foot and ten thousand horse laid siege to Granada.

The knight, Musa, led a valiant defence. He rallied the citizens, telling them, "We have nothing to fight for but the ground we stand on; without that we are without home or country." But, as at Málaga, famine did the work that cannon and gunpowder could not. On 25 November 1491, Boabdil signed the act of capitulation, giving him two months' grace to hand over the keys of the city.

The citizens lived a frenzy of desperation. Well they knew that, when Ferdinand entered Málaga, he had refused to accept the city's surrender and took the people into slavery and burned renegades alive.

Ayesha's brothers came to Don Vincent, begging him to intercede for them.

"Worry not," he said. "Our Emir has reached terms with the Catholic Kings for a *convivencia,* live and let live. Nobody will be put to the sword or enslaved. Their Majesties Ferdinand and Isabella have sworn our Islamic faith will be respected. No one will be forced to convert to Christianity, not even those like me who were born Christian. Our lives should continue, much as before."

In truth, Don Vincent was not so sure. As the due date for the handover of the city drew close, he noticed the stealthy appearance of strangers in the narrow lanes of the Al-bayyazin. These, he guessed, were the advance guard of the Catholics, smuggled into the city to forestall rebellion. If Ferdinand and Isabella feared treachery, he reasoned, perhaps this meant they had treachery on their own minds.

"Time to pick a side," the night watchman Tomaz whispered in his ear.

Each day with Ayesha was a last bounty, and he peeled and sucked every moment as if it were a pomegranate. The couple made love, prepared feasts together of their dwindling stock of grain, and he told her stories and sang her songs. He recited:

> Let us roll all our strength and all
> Our sweetness up into one ball,
> And tear our pleasures with rough strife
> Through the iron gates of life:
> Thus, though we cannot make our sun
> Stand still, yet we will make him run.

And Ayesha banished her fear of the future and dwelt with him in the coursing present. They loved with urgency, but with languid pleasure, as if they had all the time in creation.

On 2 January 1492, a world ended and a new world began. Boabdil yielded the keys of Granada to the Catholic Kings and set off up the Sierra Nevada to the tiny mountain principality of Alpujarras, which the victors had granted him. He turned for a last look at the grandeur of Granada spread out below him and shed a tear.

Don Vincent held Ayesha close, watching dumbly as the cavalcade of Castilian knights rode in to take possession of the final fragment of Moorish Spain. Ferdinand and Isabella kept their word. The couple were free to live as always, and Don Vincent found a ready audience for his recitals among the Spaniards. The city was not sacked, and its inhabitants were not forcibly converted.

Not at once, anyhow. The Jews were expelled that year. In 1493, Boabdil found intolerable his position as a vassal in Alpujarras and went into exile in Morocco.

Perhaps it was this which emboldened Cardinal Cisneros. Seven years after the conquest of the city, he accompanied the Inquisition to Granada. For him, the policy of slow and peaceful conversion of the Muslims was "giving pearls to pigs".

In violation of the Treaty of the Alhambra, signed with Boabdil, forced mass conversions followed and the ransacking of the great libraries of Granada. Five thousand Arabic manuscripts were publicly burned. Rebellion flared in the Alpujarras and was violently suppressed. Now Muslims were offered a stark choice – convert or leave Spain. Most accepted baptism, and by the year 1500, Cisneros could boast "there is now no one in the city who is not a Christian, and all the mosques are churches."

"I will not," Ayesha declared, her eyes blazing fierce. "No infidel will make me abandon the true faith."

Don Vincent knew better than to try to convince her. When the soldiers came to their house by the River Darro, she again rejected conversion.

"Let me rather die in the deserts of Africa," she said. The soldiers separated her from Don Vincent. He tried to bribe a sergeant, but the man was about God's business and shook his head.

Ayesha refused to give the conquerors the pleasure of seeing her weep as the long line of Granada's last Muslims snaked out of the city flanked by armoured conquistadores. The silence of that exodus was terrible. Don Vincent watched them go, and wept for what he had lost.

"Will you not go with your wife?" Tomaz asked.

"I am a Catholic," Don Vincent said, "and a Castilian."

At the gate of the Al-bayyazin, he saw Ayesha turn. Her hands clasped her belly. It seemed her eyes sought him out, and he fancied the Mediterranean sun glittered on tears. Her brothers never looked back.

***

The moment of betrayal is always agonising. You recite for yourself all the reasons that make it right. There's duty. There's the uncomfortable truth that you already have a wife and two vaguely C of E kids. And those are good justifications. But you can only betray what you first love.

Zami abandoned his city. At the entrance to the railway station, he looked back once and shed a tear.

INFLUENCES, THEFTS AND GRATITUDES

This is the most complex book I have ever attempted. It deals with love and betrayal, duty and madness, reality and delusion. The timeline is non-linear, because that's how memory works, especially the memory of a protagonist who seeks to justify his behaviour. Reality for Zami is the story we tell about things. Though my concerns were to show a personality fragmenting under the pressure of lies, the story is framed by a simple tale of espionage and of forbidden love. I wanted the reader to root for Zami, even though he warns you in the first chapter not to trust him. The story blends a magical tale of Moorish Spain with present-day England and psychotic figures drawn from Sumerian mythology. As Zami loses his grip on reality, the worlds bleed into each other.

In very different ways, the writing of this novel was influenced and informed by:

- News coverage in 2015 about under-cover police agents having sexual relationships with their quarries in the environment movement.

This followed the scandal of police spying on the Lawrence family. An official enquiry was set up and now, dogged by controversy and the withdrawal of collaboration by victims, limps towards the delayed opening of hearings.
- Jean Clottes book *What is Palaeolithic Art?* from which many of the rules of Zami's parallel universe were taken.
- For the portrayal of Zami's psychosis, I drew on many sources, but I owe a particular debt of gratitude to the research which informed the computer game *Hellblade; Senua's Sacrifice* by Ninja Theory.
- *Songs from the Laughing Tree* by A.U. Latif, from which I began to learn how to write magic and from which I stole the merchant selling time.
- Innumerable books and articles about Islam, the literature of so-called Islamic State, and about Moorish Granada.
- Several stories and poems which I appropriated, including, of course the tale of Khosrow and Shirin, the legend of Don Vincent which forms the basis of the first Don Vincent story and Andrew Marvell's poem *To His Coy Mistress*.

Sadly, I have lost my original notes on the story outline, so I can no longer reconstruct exactly how the novel got to this point. All that remains is a structural diagram of Byzantine complexity which I can no longer interpret.

For motivating me to complete the novel, when I had abandoned it, I have to thank the authors Claire Fuller and Paula Bonilla. My wonderful friend Jane Gibreel kindly checked the text for theological and customary mistakes, though of course, I remain responsible for any remaining errors.

The book won two prizes before it saw the light of day. The first, for the outline, came from the Plot of Gold competition in 2017. The second was a year's mentorship from Cinnamon Press. Though we didn't agree on everything, the book is as it is thanks to my mentor Adam Craig.

Adam has always felt that I've made a mistake in the first chapter by preventing readers immersing themselves. I accepted that this was running a risk, but I've always maintained that, because the book is about lies (or storytelling, depending on how you choose to look at it), it's important that the reader is provoked to think consciously about the nature of storytelling. The playwright, Brecht, used a similar technique, which he called "alienation", in his work.

I tested how great was this risk with members of the online writing community Scribophile, They, including Gabriel Stephenson and Alina Voyce, were generous with their time and critiques, and evidence that the book worked, despite any lumpiness in the first chapter.

Adam reassured me that it is still possible to sell "slim volumes". While the length of this book would not have been remarkable in the period 1850 to 1950, long-haul air travel seems to have led modern readers to expect something more like a door-stop. I am confident this book is the length it wants to be.

The tale benefitted immensely from a critical reading by Ben Evans. He persuaded me against my worse judgement to clarify the point from which the story is told and to add the descent by Zami into outright collusion in the chapters where he agrees to undertake reconnaissance of Sandhurst Military Academy.

And finally, for early encouragement and appreciative reading, my thanks go to members of my writing group, *the Fellowship of the Pen*.

March 2020